"I suppose it didn't occur to you that you could fall in love with me," he said in a lethally sexy voice.

She swallowed over a knot of denial. "It's not likely," she said.

He tilted his head to one side. "Why is that, *cherie?*"

Her nerve endings were still leap-frogging over themselves, but she refused to give in to the situation. "Because I've never fallen in love before. Why on earth would I start with you?"

He laughed, which infuriated her. "Do you think it will be that easy?"

"We're both adults," she said, pushing aside her doubts. "I've had to exercise mind over matter many times during my life. Let's shake on it."

He took her hand, but instead of shaking it, he shook his head. Then he lifted her hand and turned it so her wrist was open and vulnerable. He pressed his mouth against her and she felt her pulse jump. "Sorry, Eve, I don't make promises I don't intend to keep."

Dear Reader,

It's almost May! One of my favorite months of the year, May means birthdays, babies, Mother's Day and the return of warm weather. Add in all those wonderful spring flowers and I'm as happy as a clam. Another reason for my happiness is *The Prince's Texas Bride*.

You may remember Prince Stefan Devereaux from *Royal Holiday Baby*. Well, the truth is, Stefan is a strong man who can, on occasion, be a pain in the patootie. I took one look at him and knew what he really needed was a strong woman who didn't give a flying fig about his title. Eve Jackson is just that woman. When Stefan hires Eve to get his royal stables in order, he has no idea how quickly Eve will get under his skin straight to his soul. When his life takes a screeching unexpected turn, Eve encourages him to be his best self. You'll see. Stefan learns that having Eve in his life is not optional, it's mandatory. But can he convince a woman who insists she's not princess material that she is the queen of his heart?

Enjoy this story! It's my big hug to you to start off the magnificent month of May!

xo,

Leanne Banks

THE PRINCE'S
TEXAS BRIDE

LEANNE BANKS

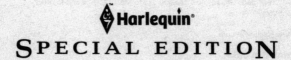

SPECIAL EDITION

ISBN-13: 978-0-373-65597-7

THE PRINCE'S TEXAS BRIDE

Books by Leanne Banks

Special Edition

Royal Holiday Baby #2075
The Prince's Texas Bride #2115

Desire

*Royal Dad #1400
Tall, Dark & Royal #1412
*His Majesty, M.D. #1435
The Playboy & Plain Jane #1483
*Princess in His Bed #1515
Between Duty and Desire #1599
Shocking the Senator #1621
Billionaire's Proposition #1699
†Bedded by the Billionaire #1863
†Billionaire's Marriage Bargain #1886
Blackmailed Into a Fake Engagement #1916
†Billionaire Extraordinaire #1939
From Playboy to Papa! #1987
**The Playboy's Proposition #1995
**Secrets of the Playboy's Bride #2002
CEO's Expectant Secretary #2018

*The Royal Dumonts
†The Billionaires Club
**The Medici Men

LEANNE BANKS

is a *New York Times* and *USA TODAY* bestselling author who is surprised every time she realizes how many books she has written. Leanne loves chocolate, the beach and new adventures. To name a few, Leanne has ridden on an elephant, stood on an ostrich egg (no, it didn't break), gone parasailing and indoor skydiving. Leanne loves writing romance because she believes in the power and magic of love. She lives in Virginia with her family and four-and-a-half-pound Pomeranian named Bijou. Visit her website at www.leannebanks.com.

This book is dedicated to Doris and Bud Banks.
Thank you for all your love and support
and for teaching us the game chicken scratch!

Prologue

The full moon wasn't offering any answers.

Eve Jackson sat in the small palace courtyard and drank in the scent of blooming flowers and ocean air as she debated the most recent offer she'd received from the official representative of the Royal House of Devereaux. She still wasn't sure she could possibly fit in as the chief stable master for the royal horses. She was from Texas, for Pete's sake, and had never traveled out of the States before this week. She'd been raised to say "yes, ma'am" and "no, sir," but the idea of performing a curtsy made her laugh every time she even thought of it.

The lure of the job, however, was too tempting for words. Her current job as a regional manager for a major hotel chain bored her so much that there were days she was tempted to poke herself in the eye with a pencil. Training horses was her first love, but when Eve had received the opportunity to go to college, she'd chosen a practical, marketable degree. Her parents had been so poor that she'd been sent off to her Aunt Hildie for most of her teen years.

Training this stable of horses was her dream job and she'd been offered a startling amount of money to do it. But she wondered if she could be happy here in a place and culture so far removed from rural Texas. And there was another concern. She felt a shift of air against her skin and her nerve endings prickled in awareness. She wasn't alone. Glancing around, she saw Prince Stefan Devereaux, tall with his chiseled features unsoftened by the moonlight, watching her from just a few feet away.

Crap, she thought, trying to remember what the proper protocol was for greeting the ruler of Chantaine. She stood because she figured she wasn't supposed to remain seated. *Crap,* she thought again. Was *he* supposed to speak first? It seemed rude to just stare back at him.

"Hi, Your Highness," she said. "How's it going?"

His lips twitched and he moved toward her. "Fine, thank you, Ms. Jackson. I hope you're enjoying your visit to my country."

"It's beautiful," she said. "Though much smaller than Texas. Not that there's anything wrong with that," she rushed to say, in case he thought she was insulting his country.

"Yes, it is, to both of your observations. My representative told me he presented you with the latest offer, but you haven't given him an answer," Stefan said. "The terms are generous. Why haven't you accepted?"

Demanding and direct, she thought, but she supposed he had the right. This was the third offer his representative had made to her, and the palace was paying for her trip to Chantaine. Eve had met Prince Stefan Devereaux of Chantaine on two other occasions. Both times, he'd surprised her. From his sister Tina, Eve had gotten the impression that he was a pompous prig. He was. For some reason, she'd also expected him to be prissy and ignorant. He was neither.

"Are you uneasy about living so far from your home?" he asked and paused a half beat. "I was under the impression you were more adventurous than that."

She lifted her chin at the subtle challenge in his tone. "It's a big move. I have to make sure it's the right one."

"You don't have children or a husband. You're young and free. What's holding you back?" he asked. "Or is there another concern?" He studied her for a moment. "If there is, you must tell me. If you're not going to accept the offer, we need to know. I must fill this position. My horses deserve consistent care."

"Your country is beautiful. I want to work with your horses," she said and decided to blurt it out. "I'm just not sure about this royal thing. I'm not big on the curtsy and I'm likely to mess up how to address you and others."

"No need to curtsy unless it's a public situation. I can have one of the advisers prompt you if necessary. When you and I are alone, you may call me Stefan. In public, it's Your Highness. It's quite simple," he said dismissively. "What else?"

"I'm not sure about the chain of command. Who is my boss? Your aide or you?"

"I am," he said. "I may deliver instructions through an assistant, but you answer to me. If you have any questions or concerns, you may approach me directly if I'm available. Anything else?" he asked, a faint thread of impatience sliding into his voice.

"Just one thing," she said, meeting his gaze but preparing herself for a big, fat turndown. "If you choose to fire me, I want six months' pay and my airfare back to the States."

His Royal Highness blinked. "Why would you request such a thing?"

"What happened to your last stable master?"

"He was fired because he wasn't doing his job properly," Stefan said.

"And the one before?" she asked.

"He was fired for negligence." Stefan narrowed his eyes. "Are you suggesting I'm a difficult employer?"

"I'm suggesting that when prized horses, powerful men and women grow accustomed to getting their way they can become...temperamental."

Stefan met her gaze and his lips twitched once again. "I don't recall ever being compared to a prized horse, but I'll choose to take it as a compliment. I'll meet your conditions if you'll meet mine. You must move to Chantaine within two weeks."

Chapter One

Day two of palace orientation and Eve's eyes were glazing over.

"Wait for His Royal Highness to address you first. Wait for His Royal Highness to extend his hand first. If you are wearing gloves when greeting His Royal Highness, you need not remove them first. Women need not wear hats before 6:30 p.m.," the elderly male adviser droned on. "Call the prince by Your Royal Highness on first meeting. Thereafter, if the conversation continues, refer to him as 'sir.' Stand whenever a royal enters the room. Never turn one's back on a royal...."

"Oh, Jonathan, give the poor girl a break," a young woman said from behind Eve.

Eve whipped her head around, spotting Princess Bridget, whom she'd met during her previous visit to Chantaine. She remembered the underlying, not-quite-buried impatience she'd sensed when she'd met Princess Bridget, a young woman close to her age.

Eve immediately rose and attempted an awkward curtsy.

Princess Bridget waved the gesture aside and tossed her head of brown, wavy hair. "Please don't. Will you join me for lunch? I need a royal break," she said. "We can discuss American reality shows."

"Your Highness," Eve said, *trying* to follow the rules she'd just been given.

"Stop, stop," Bridget said, taking Eve's hand and pulling her away. "And if you dare call me ma'am, I'll scream the palace walls down. Please call me Bridget. I'm counting on you to forget everything you've learned today so that you and I can become great friends. Thank God we have an American around now. You're just what we need."

Eve felt a combination of relief at getting away from the interminable orientation session and anxiety at Princess Bridget's plans for her. "I don't really watch a lot of reality TV."

"Well, I'm sure we'll come up with something. You know, ever since Tina got pregnant and left Chantaine, I have to do most of the public appearances." Bridget stopped and met Eve's gaze. "I'm not well suited for this. Tina was born and bred for this job. It drives me crazy."

"What specifically about the job drives you crazy?" Eve asked.

Bridget paused, blinking. Her eyebrows knitted in a frown. "I haven't thought about that. I've just been so resentful to be thrust into this right when I was enjoying my time in Italy."

Eve nodded. "I hated my last job, but it paid very well.

After working in that position, I realized that being able to do something that was my passion every day was a gift, if not a luxury."

Bridget paused again. "How profound. And I was hoping you would be a rebel."

Eve chuckled. "I am a rebel. I just try to be smart about it."

"Hmm," Bridget said. "Maybe I can learn from you. I think we should have champagne for lunch to celebrate your arrival. Dom Pérignon. If Stefan finds out, he'll be livid. I do so love to make him livid."

"No champagne for me. I don't want to start my second day on the job making my boss livid."

Bridget gave a pout and sighed. "You have a point. It wouldn't do for him to fire you right off the bat. Chardonnay?"

"And water, please," Eve said, thinking she definitely needed to remain sober around these Devereaux.

Bridget led her to a small table on a balcony that overlooked the east end of the palace grounds. Floral gardens were surrounded by lush, green grounds with trees that transitioned to rocky cliffs and sandy beaches. The ocean was a mouthwatering shade of azure.

"Beautiful view," Eve said, shaking her head in wonder. "Stunning."

Bridget stared out the window and nodded. "Yes, it is, but it can be a bit confining being surrounded by all that water. No easy way out," she said, then shrugged. "Can't change that at the moment." A staff member approached the table with a pitcher of water and filled two glasses. "Thank you, Claire. Could you also bring us a nice bottle of Chardonnay? Is lemon-roasted chicken and a green salad okay with you?" she asked Eve.

"That would be great, thanks," Eve said, swallowing

a secret laugh over the fact that she'd probably be eating peanut butter and jelly on the run if she were at the Logan Ranch.

Bridget met her gaze. "What are your interests? Besides horses, of course," she said. "Do you like to shop? Do you like music? Art?"

"Yes to music and art. I'm more fickle when it comes to shopping. With my new position here, I imagine I'll be busy enough in the beginning that I'll be getting most of my music fix from my iPod. What about you? Are there times of the year that are busier than others?"

"It seems as if it's always busy since Tina left, but I'm dragging my other sister and brother to participate in the royal appearances more often. I keep nagging Stefan for a vacation, but I think he's afraid once he lets me off the island, I'll never return," she said with a laugh.

"I apologize for my lack of knowledge, but does Chantaine have museums?"

"Two," Bridget said, not hiding her disapproval. "I've tried to talk Stefan into expanding, but he insists that both parliament and the citizens would balk when so many of our people are struggling economically."

Eve nodded, her mind wandering the way it often seemed to do whenever someone presented her with a problem. "It might go over with everyone better if you could make it a children's museum," she mused, and took a sip of her water.

Bridget stared at her for a moment. "That's a brilliant idea. If you're this brilliant about everything, it's no wonder Stefan was so intent on hiring you. You're right about starting out with a heavy workload, though," she said sympathetically. "I just remembered there's a parade in three weeks. The royal horses are featured, ridden by several top leaders and advisers."

Eve swallowed her water the wrong way and choked. "Three weeks?" she echoed.

Bridget nodded in commiseration. "Yes, and I can't help but believe that the horses are a little green." She shuddered delicately. "I hate the image of Count Christo being thrown. He's eighty-two years old. Sweet man, a little daft. He always insists on bringing a whip with him when he rides in the parade."

Eve felt her heart sink to her feet. "A whip?" she said, appalled, then sucked in a breath of air. "A *whip*," she said again, her voice rising.

Bridget shot Eve a cautious glance. "He hasn't ever actually used it."

"But he carries it," Eve said, distressed. She'd learned the uselessness of whips a long time ago.

"He's an old man," Bridget whispered. "It gives him a false feeling of control."

Eve took another deep breath and clenched her fists in her lap. More than anything, she wanted to run to the stables and begin her work with the horses. More than ever the rest of this palace protocol and orientation seemed like horse crap. She didn't want to waste one more second. Glancing at Bridget, she saw that dashing away from the princess wouldn't be possible. She clenched her fists again then released them, resolving that she would head for the stables as soon as the meal was done.

Hours later, after Eve had skipped the afternoon orientation session, she worked with a third of the many palace horses. This one was a gentle palomino mare that, like the others, hadn't been ridden often enough. She pushed down her anger that the horses hadn't been exercised. Yet, at the same time, she knew Stefan had been stalling. For her.

A smidge of guilt mixed in with her anger.

The scent of horseflesh reached her on a cellular level as she reined in the palomino. The horse submitted to her, but Eve felt the mare's urge to run. She would need to ride most of the horses once a day, if not twice during the next weeks. And the whip—God help her. How was she going to get the whip away from Count Christo?

Eve returned the mare to her stall and walked to the separate building that housed the stallion. Black was Arabian and quite the handful. She would work with him first thing in the morning, she decided as she leaned against the wall opposite his stall where he paced restlessly. The good news was that he wasn't beating down the walls of the barn.

She felt more than heard footsteps approaching and, even before she turned, her nerve endings went on alert. Turning, she saw Stefan's strong, tall form. Emanating a restless energy and power that reminded her of the stallion, he wore black riding pants and a half-buttoned shirt. His gaze was intent. "I'm the only one who rides Black," he said.

Eve refused to be intimidated. This was her job now. She would own it. "How often do you ride him?"

"Two or three times a week," he said. "Hard."

"He needs a minimum of five times per week," she told him. "Look at how restless he is."

"That's because he's a stallion," Stefan said. "Are you questioning my treatment of the horse?"

"Of course," she said. "That's why you hired me."

His mouth lifted in a half grin. "We'll do Black my way."

"For a week," she said. "If he's still restless, he'll be ridden more often, and I'll be the one riding him."

Stefan chuckled. "You?" He shook his head. "He's too much for you to handle. He was too much for the previous two men to handle."

"We'll see," she said, confident she could handle Black. She was not nearly as confident about Stefan. She watched him as he approached the stallion. The horse seemed to immediately calm. Stefan placed a bridle and saddle on the horse. He led him out of the stall, mounted him and galloped into the distance.

Chill bumps rose on her arms at the sight of man and horse flying into the moonlight. There was a mystic connection between the two of them that she couldn't deny. She felt a rush of excitement and tried to temper it with resolve. Stefan was a powerful man, but he had distractions. He wouldn't be able to ride the stallion every day. He had other demands. It wouldn't take long before she would step in as a substitute to help Black release some of his energy. Less than a week, she suspected, and she would be ready....

Exactly one week later, Stefan stared into the empty stall of his prized stallion and felt a stab of alarm. *Where is Black? Has someone let him out? Escaped?* He walked into the stall and stared at the walls. *What had—*

Realization hit him and his alarm shifted to anger. Eve had taken Black for a ride. She'd told Stefan her plans, but since he'd stated that he would be the only one to ride the stallion, he'd dismissed her statements. He'd assumed she would follow his orders. Frustration rushed through him as he glanced at his watch. He'd left his office later than usual for his ride this evening, but she still shouldn't have defied his orders.

He paced from one end of the barn to the other, his temper rising with each step. Hearing the sound of hoof-beats outside, he immediately strode to the barn door. He watched in shock as Eve swung off the stallion and led him around the corral for a cooldown. Black loped alongside her as docile as a lamb. He heard her voice, low and somehow seductive, as if she were making small talk with the stallion.

As she turned around, Black glanced upward. The horse must have caught his scent. His ears prickled and he gave a soft whinney before pulling away from Eve and trotting toward him. Stefan felt a measure of satis-faction that Black had left her behind so easily.

"There you go," Stefan said to the horse, rubbing Black's sleek throat. "I've missed you, too."

Eve, her hair escaping the long braid that hung down her back, stepped toward Black and Stefan. Her hands rested on her hips, her lips were firm and unsmiling.

"You were told not to ride him," Stefan said, delib-erately keeping his voice mild as he patted the horse.

"And I told you that he needs to be ridden more fre-quently. If you don't do it, then I will," she said. "You've only shown up twice this week. He's been so restless it's a wonder he didn't kick down the walls of his stall."

"It seems you don't understand. What I say goes about Black," he said, turning toward her.

She met his gaze. "But you still expect me to be in charge of his health, well-being, diet, etc...."

"Yes," he said, relieved the impertinent woman was beginning to understand.

She nodded. "Okay. I quit," she said and turned to walk away.

Stefan stared at her in shock, again. "Bloody hell," he muttered under his breath. "You can't quit."

She glanced over her shoulder at him. "Sure I can. You and I agreed that you would let me be in charge of running the stables. That includes Black. If you're going to interfere with me performing my job—"

"Interfere," he repeated, nearly speechless at her lack of respect. "As your employer, it's my right to agree or disagree with how you conduct your duties. Particularly in regards to Black—"

"Not if your plan isn't in the best interest of the horse," she interrupted, surprising him yet again. With the exception of his siblings, very few people interrupted him. "And as far as Black is concerned, you're not rational about him. Your insistence that you be the only one to ride him is ridiculous. You're a busy man, leader of a country for Pete's sake. You have obligations and responsibilities that are more important than making sure your favorite horse is getting enough exercise."

"I don't need you to inform me about my position. I *make* time to ride Black. It's as much for me as it is for him," he said, revealing more than he'd intended.

She stared at him for a long moment. "So is this about your ego, or about how going for a midnight ride saves you from the craziness of your position?" she asked softly.

He felt as if she'd stabbed him. What right did she have to judge him? His rides with Black were the only time he felt truly free.

"I'm not trying to step on your toes or prevent you from the pleasure of riding Black. I'm just being realistic. He's a prize of an animal, smart, powerful and fast," she said, glancing toward the horse. "But he's full of energy and if he isn't exercised more frequently he's going to be miserable. I don't think you want that."

He clenched his teeth then sucked in a quick breath. "How did you do it? No one has been able to ride him except for me."

She lifted her lips in a smile that made his gut twist. "That's my secret," she said. "I'm a horse whisperer," she said in a self-mocking tone. "That's why you hired me."

"For the others," he said.

"Hmm," she said with a nod of understanding. "Looks like you have a decision to make. Let me know by morning, and I'll take the first flight back to Texas."

He caught her wrist as she turned around and she glanced at him in surprise. "You're not getting out of the job that easily," he said. "Ride Black, but do so at your own risk. I'll let you know which nights I'll ride him."

Her gaze searched his face. "So you do have a reasonable bone or two in your body," she said.

His lips curved in amusement despite the fact that he was still irritated with her. "Of course I do. I'm forced to be reasonable day in and day out with government leaders and advisers."

"Which is why you really need those rides with Black," she said.

Her perceptiveness was both a bother and a relief. There weren't many, if any, people who Stefan allowed close, and he'd been told by more than a few that he was difficult to read. The truth was that his passions always felt as if they were just beneath the surface, ready to burst through, so he felt he had to exert enormous self-control.

Gazing down at her, he saw a combination of

compassion and challenge in her dark eyes. Her lips were pursed as if she were trying not to smile. His hand still encircled her wrist and the skin there felt soft in contrast to her spine of steel. What an odd mix of a woman, he thought. He wondered what she was like in bed. He wondered what she would do if he kissed her. A hot visual of her naked beneath him whipped through his mind.

His immediate surge of desire took him by surprise. Eve wasn't his type. She was argumentative. She had zero understanding of palace affairs. For God's sake, she worked in a barn. In that flash of an instant, he glimpsed a shot of awareness that deepened her already dark eyes. In the next second, he saw the same surprise he'd felt.

Taking a breath, she stepped back and pulled her hand from his. "If you can let me know by 8:00 p.m. on the nights you'll be riding him, that would help me," she said.

"Waiting till that late will tie up most of your evenings," he said.

"I don't have anything else on my calendar. You see, I have to get ready for this parade my boss neglected to tell me about," she said in a confiding tone.

"That's why I required you to come to Chantaine within two weeks," Stefan said, mildly amused.

"It would have been nice of you to let me know ahead of time," she said.

"I'm not that nice," he said. "Would it have made a difference?"

"I guess not," she said. "I just wouldn't have sat through any of those orientation sessions," she said.

"I was told you skipped the afternoon session," Stefan said.

"That's true," she said. "As soon as Princess Bridget

told me there was going to be a parade with some kook waving a whip, I was outta there."

"Count Christo is eccentric, but I wouldn't call him a kook," Stefan said.

"You don't have to," Eve said. "And I'll tell you now, he won't be carrying a whip when he's riding one of your horses."

"Eve," Stefan said. "The count is an important and revered member of Chantaine society."

"He won't even miss that whip, I promise," she said.

"Eve," he said again.

She waved her hand in dismissal. "That's a week and a half away. No worries Your Highlyness," she said with a sparkle in her eye.

"Highlyness?" he echoed.

"That's what my aunt Hildie calls Tina every now and then."

The tidbit amused him. "I bet Tina loved that."

"Oh, you have no idea," she said and gave a pretty little salute with her right hand. "I should hit the sack, Your Highlyness. I rise early these days. Sweet dreams."

The next day as Eve was grabbing a sandwich at her office in the stables, she mulled over the possibility of providing Black with a companion. The stallion led such a solitary life he might be more content with a gelding as a friend, or perhaps a goat.

"There you are," Bridget, wearing a dress and heels, said from the doorway. She walked inside the small office without invitation, wagging her finger in disapproval. "You've been invisible during the last week. I was certain you'd flown back to Texas until I overheard one of the staff discussing how early you leave your quarters in the morning and how late you return at night. You're going to exhaust yourself before you've even been here a month, and Tina will have all our heads. This must stop."

Despite Bridget's propensity for exaggeration, Eve felt a little less alone by her presence. She'd been so busy with the horses that she hadn't had time to think about anything else except late at night before she fell asleep. She would die before she admitted it, but she was a little homesick.

"I'm fine," Eve insisted and set down her sandwich. "I just needed to jump in with both feet with the parade coming around the corner."

"Well, it's simply not acceptable," Bridget said. "I'm sure you haven't even taken off one day since you arrived. Therefore, you shall go shopping with me this afternoon," she said in full princess mode.

Eve shook her head. "It's sweet of you to ask, and I'm honored, but I can't. It would just put me behind. I have to start scheduling appointments with the riders so everything will go smoothly during the parade."

Bridget wrinkled her brow in confusion. "We've never had appointments before. We just show up on parade day, mount the horse and ride."

"How did that work out?" Eve asked, already knowing the answer.

"Fine with me. There have been a few little problems. One of the mares bucked her rider and took off through the crowd. One of the geldings stopped halfway through and refused to go any farther."

"And what about that year when one of the horses reared up and a half dozen of them went to the beach? Not just to the beach," Eve said. "But in the water."

Bridget winced. "Oh, yes. I couldn't really blame

them. It was a very hot day and the master of ceremonies was long-winded, which meant we had to wait forever to get started. I guess you're right. Good luck getting some of the old guys to agree to the appointments, though."

"Thank you," Eve said in a long-suffering voice.

Bridget sighed. "Well, if you won't go shopping with me, then you must join us for dinner tonight. It's family night. Stefan requires us to have dinner together every week since Jacques is on break from college. He'll be there as well as Phillipa."

Eve immediately began to shake her head. "I'm not family. I wouldn't want to intrude," she said, also confident that she would feel totally out of place at a table full of royals.

"No intrusion," Bridget said. "Besides, you're like family because of your association with Tina."

"Oh, no, thank you, but—"

"I won't take no for an answer. You must eat. You may as well eat with us. The food will be better than that sandwich," she said, waving her hand in disgust at Eve's lunch. "If you don't come, then I'll have to tell Tina, and she'll fuss at Stefan and me. Trust me, it will get messy."

Eve sighed, realizing it would be easier to give in to Bridget's invitation and beg off early. She could pretend to be a fly on the wall and resolved to keep her mouth shut. "If you insist," she said.

"I do," Bridget said, smiling broadly. "We'll dine at seven on the third floor. It's a bit smaller and more intimate. I'm delighted you'll join us. Ta-ta," she said and turned to leave.

"Bridget," Eve said before the woman vanished. Geez, that woman could move like the wind despite the fact that she was wearing high heels. "What should I wear?"

Bridget glanced over her shoulder. "Oh, it's not formal. Just a dress will do."

Eve had brought only a few dresses with her since she figured she would be spending most of her time with the horses. Her choices were black, brown and black. She decided on black and pulled her hair out of her braid. For her corporate job back in the States, she'd always dressed in a conservative, businesslike manner, with careful attention to grooming.

Looking in the mirror made her wince. She'd been so focused on getting the horses ready for the parade that she'd done the bare minimum in the grooming department. Her fingernails were all broken down to the quick, her hair was out of control, her lips were chapped and smudges of violet rimmed her brown eyes.

"Thank goodness for concealer," she muttered under her breath, then got to work. Nerves danced in her belly and she chastised herself. She shouldn't be nervous. Although she'd never shared a meal with a roomful of royals, she knew which fork to use and when. Her aunt Hildie had made sure she knew her manners. Eve felt a jab of homesickness take her by surprise, then pushed it down. It wasn't as if she were being sent away from her parents when she'd become a teenager. She'd made this choice of her own volition. She was here for her dream job.

The prospect of interacting with Stefan on a semisocial level still made her uncomfortable. She was at ease dealing with him over matters concerning the horses, but beyond that, she found the man unsettling. After hearing his sister Tina talk about how overbearing he was, she'd

been certain she'd find him a selfish chauvinist. But she
was beginning to see that he was far more complex than
she'd first thought. He had a lot on his shoulders and he
didn't shift one bit under his responsibilities. To her, it
appeared that he was trying to bring the siblings together
for the sake of Chantaine, and the independent-minded
Devereaux weren't making it easy.

Eve finished getting dressed and walked from the
staff quarters to the palace. A guard allowed her entrance, and she climbed the marble steps to the third
floor and wandered down the long hallway to an open
doorway from where she heard voices—Bridget's in
particular.

Eve peeked around the corner and caught her first
glimpse of the lavish dining room. With a different table,
the room could have easily held twenty people. Instead,
a round table dressed in a crisp white cloth and set with
crystal glasses, sterling silver and bone china sat in the
center of the room.

The elegance and luxury of the room reminded her
of the differences between her background and that of
the Devereaux family. Her parents had moved frequently
to stay a step ahead of the debt collectors, which meant
she'd never stayed in one school very long. A flood
of memories washed over her of walking into school,
wearing clothes with holes in them, suffering the stares
of her classmates and feeling completely out of place.

Her stomach knotted. What was she doing here? She
took a deep breath and told herself this was a different
time, a different situation. The siblings distracted her
from her panic.

Bridget, Phillipa and Jacques stood beside the table.

"The goal for this evening's meal is to get Stefan to

cut me some slack," Bridget said. "I need a vacation in Italy. Phillipa, you can cover for me for just a couple weeks—"

Phillipa shook her head. "You know I'm in the middle of my dissertation. I can't take off for two weeks."

Bridget sighed. "Maybe we could cut down some of the appearances." She glanced at Jacques, who bore a striking resemblance to Stefan. "And you could help."

Jacques looked appalled. "Me? I'm playing in a soccer match in Spain this weekend."

"Well, I can't keep doing all this on my own. Lord knows how Tina managed it," Bridget said.

Eve strongly considered turning around and leaving at that point, but Jacques glanced up and looked at her as if she were a lifeline. "Please do come in. Eve Jackson?"

"Yes, Your Highness," she said. "I'm surprised you remember since we met so briefly last month."

Jacques's lips lifted in a flirtatious grin. "Please call me Jacques, and I make a habit of never forgetting the name of a beautiful woman."

Eve couldn't resist smiling in return. She could tell Jacques was on the road to be a class-one heartbreaker. "Thank you, Jacques. I appreciate the flattery, especially since I haven't spent much time outside the barn since I arrived."

"I'm determined to change that," Bridget said. "Just because your position requires you to work with the horses doesn't mean you're married to them. Tomorrow you can join me for a day at the beach."

Eve shook her head. "No beach for me until after the parade."

Bridget scowled. "Tina is going to—" She broke off as Stefan walked into the room. "Welcome, Stefan. I persuaded Eve to join us tonight. She's been cooped up in the barn far too long. I'm sure you don't mind."

Eve blinked at that last remark, feeling a stab of chagrin. She'd assumed Stefan had already been informed and approved of her presence at the meal.

Stefan looked at her, his gaze falling over her from head to toe and back up again. "Of course not. I'm glad you thought of it, Bridget," he said, his gaze not straying from Eve's. "Our pleasure, Eve."

"Thank you, Your High—" she started, but stopped when he sliced his hand through the air.

"Stefan, please. Shall we sit?"

As if on cue, three staff members immediately entered the room.

"I chose Chateaubriand for the menu tonight," Bridget said. "I asked the chef to choose everything else…well, aside from the chocolate mousse torte. Do you like chocolate, Eve?"

Still self-conscious, Eve fidgeted with her hands in her lap. "*Like* is an understatement. I've been known to make dessert the main course when it's chocolate."

Bridget laughed in approval. "Well, you won't want to skip any of the courses tonight. Our newest chef is fabulous."

"Here, here," Jacques said. "Much improved over food at the university."

Eve lifted her water glass and took a swallow. "Newest," she echoed. "How new is he?"

Bridget glanced at Stefan. "Three months, would you say? The employment director had to replace the former chef."

Hiding a grin of amusement behind her glass, Eve took another sip and met Stefan's gaze. "Is that so?"

He raised a dark eyebrow as if he knew exactly what

she was thinking. "The employment director made that decision. I had nothing to do with it."

"Oh, I know why he was dismissed," Phillipa said. "He was coming to work later and later due to a drinking problem. The employment director set him up with a special rehabilitation program."

Stefan lifted his glass of wine, his lips twitching in amusement before he took a sip. "Eve seems to be under the misguided impression that I fire so many staff members we may as well have a revolving door for them."

All four Devereaux stared at her with questions in their eyes. Eve coughed as her water went down the wrong way.

"What on earth made you think that?" Phillipa asked. "Stefan delegates almost all of the hiring to the employment director."

"I never said that. I—" The gleam in his eyes told her he was enjoying her discomfort far too much. Eve frowned at Stefan, rising to the challenge. She was a Texan, for Pete's sake, and she refused to be intimidated. "How many horse managers have you gone through? How long did my predecessor last before you bumped him off?"

Shocked silence followed, and Eve lifted her chin even as she felt herself being stared down by everyone in the room.

Stefan's bark of laughter broke the silence and the tension. "To Americans," he said and lifted his glass. "You don't take crap from anyone."

Stefan's siblings gaped at her in surprise. Bridget recovered first, lifting her glass in salute. "We can learn by her example."

Stefan lifted his hand in disagreement. "There's a

difference between defending oneself and constantly quarreling."

"But, Stefan—"

"Enough, Bridget," he said and turned to Phillipa. "How are your studies progressing?"

Stefan held her attention with how he conducted himself. He exhibited a magnetism that combined power, intelligence and complete masculinity. She'd never met a man who possessed such a combination. She was accustomed to sly cowboys and corporate managers with egos bigger than their paychecks.

She studied his hands as he cut his beef and lifted his glass of wine to his lips. His fingers were long, and she remembered feeling the faintest bit of a callous in his palms when he'd shaken her hand. She'd liked that about him.

Now, as she watched him talking to his siblings, she liked the way he focused on them instead of himself. She wondered if he kept his concerns and worries from his siblings. She wondered if he'd protected them a bit too much.

"If everything works out, I may do an exchange course in Italy this summer. Florence," Jacques said with a half grin. "My advisers say I'm spending enough time on soccer and they want me to be well-rounded."

"Florence," Bridget muttered and gave a low, barely audible growl. She cleared her throat. "Speaking of art, Eve and I were talking just a couple of weeks ago about the idea of building a children's art museum in Chantaine."

Eve cringed at being dragged into Bridget's power struggle with Stefan.

"Bridget, you know the agreement about our family dinners," Stefan said with a sigh. "No discussion about financial proposals or arguments about politics. This is a time for us to be family."

"Well, it's hard for me to be family when all I do is work, work, work," she said. "Have you noticed that you haven't asked me anything about my personal life? Why?" she demanded. "Because I have no personal life. If I can't have a personal life, then I'd like to have a sense of satisfaction. Even Eve said being happy in your job is making sure you have a passion for what you're doing."

Eve felt Stefan's hard glare. She felt stuck in the middle of a place she absolutely didn't want to be. Lifting her glass of wine, she took a sip and latched onto the first thing that came to her mind. "Anyone here know how to play the game Chicken Scratch?"

Chapter Two

With the exception of Stefan, it had been like taking candy from a baby. Stefan had actually won the third game. Eve spread out her hands to collect the dominos. "Well, this has been fun, but I need to visit the barn one more time tonight."

"No," Jacques said. "I was just getting used to it."

"Me, too," Bridget said. "I almost won the second game."

"Afraid you'll lose again?" Stefan challenged.

Her stomach did a crazy tumble at the expression on his face. "Not at all," she said. "I really do need to visit the barn again. If you liked the game, I'll leave my dominoes here so you can practice."

"Please do," Phillipa murmured. "We need it."

Eve smiled at the brainy princess determined to master the game. "If we play again, I bet all of you will beat the pants off of me."

"I'd like to see that," Jacques said with a devilish look in his eyes.

"Jacques," Stefan said with a frown. "Ms. Jackson is our guest while at dinner. She deserves our respect."

"Exactly," Eve agreed. "Your elders always deserve your respect."

Jacques laughed. "If you're my elder…"

"Jacques," Stefan said again, this time a touch of amusement slid into his tone as he gave a barely perceptible shake of his head.

"Thank you all again for everything. Joining you for dinner was an—honor," she said and smiled. "Good night and sweet dreams," she said, turning to leave.

"Sweet dreams?" Phillipa echoed.

"It's an expression," Eve said. "I'm wishing you sweet dreams."

"That's lovely," Bridget said. "Sweet dreams to you, too."

"Thank you," Eve said and felt Stefan studying her. She felt a quiver of something strange in her belly and pushed it aside. "Your Highnesses," she said and walked away.

The family dinner had gone much better than usual due to Eve's presence, Stefan thought as he paced his quarters. She'd amused him by the way she'd pushed back when he'd teased her. The sound of her Texas drawl slid over his nerve endings like a smooth brandy. Her little game had distracted his family from the usual squabbles and griping, and allowed them to enjoy their time together. He would make sure she was included again.

Glancing at the clock, he thought about his early meeting with dignitaries from Russia in the morning.

It would serve him well to go to sleep, but he was too restless. Lately, he'd been even more restless than usual. Bumping up his exercise routine hadn't helped. The advisers had been pressing him more than ever on a matter that he'd avoided like the plague. But he knew they were right. He couldn't delay this part of his duty forever. He glanced out the French doors of his balcony and watched the clouds slide over the moon. Inhaling, he caught the scent of impending rain. The atmosphere felt moody. Like him, he thought with wry chagrin.

An impulse shot through him and he considered it for thirty seconds. As ruler, he'd learned early on he would have to be selective about giving in to impulses. This one would help him sleep and quiet his spirit. He changed his clothes and called his personal guard, Georg. "I'm going to ride Black."

"Yes, Your Highness. Would you like me to arrange for the horse to be saddled before you get to the barn?"

"Not necessary. I'll do it," Stefan said.

"Enjoy your ride, sir," the security guard said.

"Thank you," Stefan said and headed for the barn.

He heard her talking with Black before he looked inside the horse's stall. Black nodded as Eve talked as if he understood exactly what she was saying. "So, how do you like the idea of a goat?" she asked. "I have a feeling you would do better with a pet than another horse."

"A goat?" Stefan echoed and watched Eve whirl around in surprise. She adjusted her black Stetson. "Black would stomp the poor animal to smithereens."

"Maybe not," she disagreed, stroking the stallion in question. "By nature, horses aren't solitary animals. He's so restless. I think a pet might help him calm down."

Stefan stroked his chin. "I'll think about it," he said

and wryly wished a pet goat would solve his own restlessness. "Did you ride him this evening?"

She shook her head. "No. I just visited him because I had a feeling you might want a ride tonight."

He appreciated her perception. "Family night can be an obstacle course, but I think it's necessary."

"I agree with you. Were you and your sisters and brother ever close?"

"That's a good question," he said as he entered the stall. Black immediately approached him, and Stefan felt a rush of pleasure at the way the horse responded to his presence. "We had different assignments, different nannies, even different advisers. Tina and I shared some similar training. I think that's why we're so close. Then Fredericka had her substance abuse issues and it became a priority to make sure that none of the other Devereaux went down that same road. If anyone was the glue between us all, it was Tina. When she left, it was a terrible blow."

"Bet you're still bummed about it," Eve said, resting her hand on her hip as she studied him.

"Bummed, but mostly resigned. I'm glad she's agreed to visits," he said, feeling a pang of missing his sister.

Her lips twitched. "And now you get to deal with Bridget," she said. "My aunt would say that should be a character-building experience for both of you."

"Is this the same aunt who addressed Tina as 'Your Highlyness'?"

"The one and only Hildie," Eve said with soft smile. "She's the best."

"And you miss her," he said, reading the combination of affection tempered with sadness on her face.

Eve glanced away then lifted her chin. "Probably more than I expected, but I'm too busy to spend much time feeling homesick. Speaking of time, I shouldn't keep you from your ride. Your boy is ready for you," she said, nodding toward the stallion.

He realized he'd just been dismissed and he wasn't sure he liked it. A surge of strange feelings rumbled through him. Sympathy for Eve…curiosity…something else he couldn't name. "Would you like to join me?"

Eve blinked in surprise. "Join you?" she echoed in disbelief.

"You can bring one of the geldings. It will be a short ride tonight since the weather is threatening," he said. "If you think you're up to it," he added, deliberately challenging her.

"I'm up to it," she retorted immediately. "I'll get Gus and meet you out back."

Moments later, she joined him and Black. "Where are we going?" she asked, leaning forward to give Gus a reassuring stroke on his neck.

"The beach," Stefan said and, even in the darkness, he saw her face light up.

"I haven't ridden there yet," she said. "I've stuck to the trails on the palace grounds."

"You won't after you've ridden on the beach," he said, urging Black into a fast trot. Leaving the confines of the stable yards behind, he led Eve on a winding path through dense woods. In the past, his security had wanted to ride with him and he'd always felt it was the worst kind of intrusion. He'd known forever that his life would never be totally his, but Stefan just wanted a few moments to breathe and escape. He'd never invited anyone with him on his night rides, but tonight he'd sensed the same combination of claustrophobia and loneliness in Eve that he often felt himself. Hers came from adjusting to living on an island and homesickness. A ride on the beach might offer her the same temporary cure it did him. He pulled his horse to a stop as they entered a clearing that offered a view of the beach below.

"It's beautiful," she said in a low, but awed voice.

"Yes, it is," he agreed. "I wanted to warn you that the slope's a little steep down this hill. Black could find his way down this hill blind, but Gus may need some extra time."

"No problem. I wouldn't do it any other way," she said.

Just as Stefan had said, Black made it down the hill in no time. As soon as Black hit level ground with the beach mere yards away, Stefan could feel the stallion pulling on the reins. He knew what was coming. "Patience," he said as the horse pranced. "She'll be here in just a moment or two."

Hearing the sound of Gus's hooves behind him, he turned, expecting the gelding to stop. Instead, Eve urged the horse into a fast trot and rode right past him. "See ya!" she called with a laugh, and Gus took off.

Black gave a snort of protest as Stefan watched in surprise. Seemingly one with the horse, she rode better than any woman and most men he'd met. Exhilaration raced through him. With her hair flying behind her and her compact body huddled closely against Gus, she was pure pleasure to watch. Black pulled against the reins, and Stefan allowed him to run. It wouldn't take long to catch them.

A moment later, Black pulled alongside Eve and Gus. Eve glanced over at Stefan and her breathless laughter drifted over him with the ocean breeze. The sound of her exultation made him smile. The night was dark; a storm was on the way, but he suddenly felt as if the sun had come out from behind a cloud.

Black increased his speed and Gus struggled to keep up. "Go ahead," she called with a wave. "It's your time. Take it."

Stefan gave Black the reins and the stallion sped down the beach. He felt the rush of adrenaline punch through him. His heart raced, and he felt free. The speed and wind blew the clutter from his mind. This never got old. For Stefan, this was what got him through his worst days. Black loved this run, too. If given the chance, the horse would run around the entire island, but Stefan had made a deal with security. Another fifty yards and then he would turn back. He reined in the horse. At the turn, Black slowed even more, sensing that turning around was the beginning of the end of the ride.

In the near distance, Stefan saw Eve riding Gus at the edge of the ocean. Surprising him again, she slid off the horse, kicked off her boots and rolled up her jeans. He rode closer as she waded into the water. "Careful," he called. "The bottom drops off sharply. You don't want to get—"

She took a step and sank in up to her chest, holding on to her hat. She let out a squeal that sent a shot of alarm through him. He swung off of Black, ready to pull her from the water. But then he heard her laughter. The sound reminded him of happy bells. As she trudged out of the ocean, she tugged at her wet shirt, pulling it away from her stomach, still giggling.

"You're drenched," he said. "I tried to warn you."

She waved her hand and lifted her gaze to meet his. Even in the dark of the night, he could see her eyes glint with amusement. "It's just water. I couldn't resist. I haven't left the barn long enough to visit the ocean since I've been here. It was just too tempting and I knew Gus wouldn't go anywhere without me."

Her lack of concern over the dunking was refreshing. Every other woman he knew would have been embarrassed and disgruntled. "I never intended for you to chain yourself to the barn. You're entitled to take some time for yourself."

"Not until after the parade," she said. "I don't want these babies misbehaving when they're on my clock." She put her foot in the stirrup and began to lift herself, then stepped back on the ground, shaking her head as she pulled up her jeans. "A little heavier than usual," she murmured.

"A good soak will do that," he said in a wry tone.

"To be perfectly honest, if my boss weren't with me, I'd ditch the jeans until I got back to the barn," she said and lifted herself again.

When she wobbled, Stefan gave her an extra boost on her backside. "Don't let my presence deter you from your—comfort."

Eve glanced down at him and for an instant he felt the scorching heat of sensual assessment in her gaze. She shook her head as if she were trying to clear it. "You surprise me, Your Highness. I didn't know you were capable of flirting with your stable maid," she drawled.

"You're far more than a stable maid," he said and then mounted Black. The way she'd emphasized the difference between his position and hers irritated him. This ride represented a time out for him. He wanted no reminders of his position. Determined to hold on to the last few moments of the ride, the sea air, the breeze, the darkness, he kept the stallion moving at a trot instead of a canter. Still it was no time before he and Eve arrived at the barn. She took care of Gus while he cared for

Black. The stallion still seemed a bit restless as Stefan stepped from the stall.

He felt Eve move to his side. "He acts like he needs another ride," Eve murmured.

Stefan glanced down at her, noticing the way she rubbed her arms. The shirt was still dark from her stroll in the ocean, and he suspected her jeans were very uncomfortable. He swore under his breath. "You're still wet and I can tell you're chilled. You need to get back to your room immediately."

She wrinkled her brow in surprise and shrugged. "I'm fine. Like I said, it's just water. I'm seriously considering a goat for Black. I think—"

"Enough about Black tonight. Go to your quarters and dry off," Stefan said and, when she didn't move, the next words automatically came out of his mouth, "I command it."

Her eyes widened like saucers. "You *command* it?" she echoed in disbelief.

Stefan bit back an oath. He'd known from the beginning that Eve wouldn't respond well to orders. He rarely pulled rank. Why in hell did she bring out the urge entirely too often? He bloody well couldn't back down now. "I do."

She blinked. "I'm not sure I like that."

"It's not that difficult to understand. You insist that my horses behave correctly because they are on your clock. In a way, you are on my clock," he said. "I won't have you getting pneumonia on my watch."

"Are you comparing me to a horse?"

"No," he said. "Besides the fact that Tina would kill me if anything happened to you, I wouldn't be able to stand it myself."

"But I'm not your responsibility," she argued.

"You are in my country. Therefore, you are my responsibility."

She stared at him for a long moment and shivered. His gaze lowered to her damp shirt stretched taut over her breasts, her nipples forming a tempting outline. He felt an immediate visceral response. Instinct urged him to rub her arms with his hands, to pull her against his body and make her warm. He clenched his hands into fists. Denial had been drilled into him since the day he was born, even more so when he'd come to understand the playboy image of his father and grandfather. When he'd come of age, many people had expected that he would follow in his father's footsteps.

Stefan had wanted more. He wanted the opportunity to change and improve his country. For that, he had to be taken seriously. He'd kept his affairs scrupulously private. His duty and the sins of his father had forced him to hold his libido in check. Right now, though, for the first time in a long time, he fought the urge to pull the mouthy American Eve Jackson into his arms and make love to her against any flat surface available.

He reined in his surprising need. "I'll walk you to your quarters," he said.

"Oh, that's so not necessary. I walk to my quarters by myself every night," she said.

"You're not dripping wet every night," he said, extending his hand, determined to maintain control. "Come, now."

Eve rolled her eyes, but placed her cool hand in his. "Sheesh, did anyone ever tell you that you take this Highlyness thing a bit far?"

"No one except my sisters," he said as he led the way to the staff quarters. He rarely walked this path. Now that he saw it, he decided it needed a few more lights. "How late do you usually stay at the stables?"

She shrugged. "It depends. I usually grab a sandwich for dinner and head back around nine or ten."

"I'm not sure it's best for you to be walking back to the staff quarters unescorted every night," he said.

"Oh, give me a break. I've spent my life going anywhere I need to go unescorted. Besides, I'll bet you didn't tell your previous stable master that he shouldn't be walking around the grounds unescorted."

"Trust me, he didn't look at all like you. Plus, he never felt the necessity to work full-time let alone overtime. I prefer you leave the stables before dark for the next couple of nights. I'll get motion lights installed."

"We'll see," she muttered.

He gave a double take. "We'll see?" he echoed. "I just gave you a very reasonable order."

She sighed. "Do you really think you have criminals wandering around the palace grounds?"

"I'll admit it's not likely, and the security here is as good as it gets without causing claustrophobia, but nothing is perfect. I will be more comfortable if you avoid walking alone at night until there's more lighting."

"So this is about your comfort and not mine?" she said.

Damn, the woman was difficult, he thought. "Perhaps. You need to remember that you're not just an employee. Because of your relationship with Tina, you're also a friend of the family. We protect our friends." He noticed her fighting a shiver and swore under his breath and rubbed her arms. "I shouldn't be keeping you out in the cool air. Go inside and get warm."

Her gaze met his for a moment and he saw a shot of liquid heat flash through her eyes. He saw the possibility of passion and felt it deep in his gut. She took a quick breath and her lips parted, drawing his attention. He wondered how that argumentative mouth would feel beneath his. He wondered how she would respond.

For once, Stefan had finally met a woman who didn't give a damn about his title or position. She had no interest in pacifying him and would argue with him at the drop of a hat, yet he sensed that a part of her wanted him. Tempted, more so than he'd felt in a long time, he wondered if Eve could handle an affair with him. He suspected she met his requirement of being discreet. How messy would it be once their affair ended? Because they all ended.

She closed her eyes as if she were trying to shut down her emotions. That annoyed him. He wanted her open to him. He wanted to see the desire in her eyes again.

Taking another breath, she opened her eyes and took a step away from him. "Thanks for the night ride," she said in a husky voice that brushed over his nerve endings. "Good night."

He watched her jog inside the back door to the staff quarters and felt a surprising urge to go after her. He snuffed it out, of course. Even though Eve aroused more than his curiosity, he couldn't rush into anything. There was too much at stake to be impulsive. There always had been and there always would be.

At ten o'clock the next morning, Eve was returning one of the horses to the stall when she heard Bridget's voice.

"Bonjour, Mademoiselle Jackson," she called. "I am your rescuer and have come to help you escape your drudgery for a while."

Eve sighed, although she couldn't deny she was

amused. Bridget would do anything to get out of palace duties. She closed the door to Gus's stall. "Bridget, that's very sweet of you, but—"

"No refusals allowed," Bridget said. "You and I have received orders from on high."

Eve turned to face the princess and blinked at the sight. It was clear what the plans for the outing were from Bridget's beach cover-up, gigantic sunglasses, a large-brim, black straw hat and designer beach bag.

"Orders from on high?" Eve echoed.

Bridget nodded. "Stefan has spoken. He says you need a day off, and I've been assigned to take you to the beach." She lifted her finger. "Don't you dare fight me on this. It wasn't my idea, but it's my first opportunity to have a little fun in what must be a century. If I have to attend another charity tea, I'll scream. Besides, Stefan is right. You must take a break. Forgive me for being blunt, but you're looking a bit, well, haggard."

Eve hardly knew how to respond to Bridget's mouthful of drama. She'd already shot down Eve's objections before she'd had a chance to voice them. "I have difficulty believing the palace protests other members of the staff working too hard."

Bridget gave a *tsk*-ing sound. "Eve, other members of the staff take every possible break. Besides, you're not just staff. Tina gave you to us. The rules are different. Oh, for goodness' sake, I'm suggesting a day at the beach. Not the guillotine. Your reluctance is insulting. Do you dislike me so much?"

Eve laughed in exasperation. "I don't dislike you. I just need to stay on top of my duties. The parade is days away—"

"And everything is going to go brilliantly. In the meantime, the sun is shining and the beach is calling."

She clapped her hands lightly. "Come, come. You do have a swimsuit, don't you?

"Yes, but—"

"No buts," Bridget said.

"You Devereaux drive a hard bargain," Eve said.

"Oh, good," Bridget said. "I smell the sweet scent of surrender. Don't worry about sunscreen. I have plenty. Move along."

Within forty-five minutes, Eve and Bridget were reclining in lounge chairs on a semi-private beach where, magically it seemed, servers appeared to deliver refreshing beverages and snacks.

"Are you sure you don't want more than water?" Bridget asked.

"For now," Eve said, closing her eyes and enjoying the feeling of sunshine and gentle ocean breeze over her skin. "You and Stefan were right. I needed this."

"Of course I was right," Bridget said, neatly eliminating Stefan from the equation. "The staff has prepared lunch. We can eat in an hour or two. They'll also be putting up umbrellas soon. It has occurred to me that you've been too busy to make new friends in Chantaine since you arrived. In the same vein, you haven't had the opportunity to meet any men. While I'll confess that the selection is much better in Europe than here," Bridget said in a dry voice, "I could introduce you to someone who could amuse you. You and I could visit one of our nightclubs."

"Not my thing," Eve said, keeping her eyes closed.

"Why ever not? What do you do for fun?"

"I enjoy riding and taking care of horses. I enjoy the beach. I like to read. I like to play card games and Chicken Scratch—"

"Oh, well, I can agree with Chicken Scratch. We are

all determined to have you return for family dinner night and another round of it," Bridget said.

"Great," Eve said wryly. "I can't wait to have the entire Devereaux dynasty gang up on me."

Bridget laughed. "It's your fault. You started it."

"I thought this was supposed to help me relax," Eve muttered, but focused on the sound of the ocean waves. She cautioned herself not to get used to it, but this was bliss. She drifted off....

"Is she getting too much sun?"

The voice, which seemed to affect her on a cellular level, awakened her with no warning and she sat up, disoriented. "What?"

The tall, strong body of Prince Stefan towered over her, casting a long shadow. Eve covered her eyes at the bright sunlight.

"Not at all. She applied sunscreen, and the staff put up an umbrella to shield her. Poor thing must be dead tired. She's been asleep for the last half hour. Stefan, you're working her too hard," Bridget said.

"It's not me," he said. "She insists on working from before dawn to after dusk. The American way."

Eve drew in a mind-clearing breath and tried to dismiss the effect Stefan had on her. She noticed he was dressed in a dark suit and the contrast with the white sand distracted her. She wondered how he would look wearing just a swim suit. Or less. "I'm awake now. You can talk *to* me instead of *about* me."

Bridget giggled. "I tried to talk Eve into going to a nightclub with me, but she wasn't interested. You should wave your imperial wand, Stefan. That was the only way I was able to persuade her to join me at the beach. I'm sure Tina would want to make sure we're introducing her to new friends, including new male friends."

"Perhaps Eve isn't interested in the kind of men she would meet at a club," Stefan said.

"Won't know till she tries," Bridget said in an airy voice. "However, I would be more than willing to escort her to Italy. I have the perfect club selected for tonight, thought—"

"I couldn't be less interested in a club tonight," Eve said. "The little trip to this perfect beach has relaxed me so much it scares me. Even though I'm being a slug today, I'm certain I'll sleep like a log tonight. I think it's the sea air."

"Good to hear it," Stefan said with a nod. "The family is having an early dinner with Jacques since he will be returning this weekend. We want you to join us."

Eve slid a sideways glance at Bridget, who looked as innocent as possible in her black bikini and straw hat with a martini in her hand. "I'm sure you would prefer to keep the night to just your family. I don't want to interfere."

"We insist," Stefan said, using the royal *we*.

"This is about Chicken Scratch, isn't it?" Eve said glumly.

"My siblings are compelled to hold a rematch," Stefan said.

"Okay, okay," Eve said. "But only two games."

"That leaves no opportunity for a tiebreaker," Bridget said.

"Exactly," Eve said.

Stefan met Eve's gaze and shot her a grin that mixed challenge and sensuality. The combination sent a ripple down her spine. "I look forward to the evening," he said and walked away.

Eve sank back against her lounge and groaned. "I thought you intended this to be relaxing."

"It is," Bridget said cheerfully as she lifted her martini glass.

"How can I relax knowing I'm attending a family dinner at the palace where all of you want to rip me to shreds?" Eve asked.

"The dinner will be delicious," Bridget said. "We only want to best you at Chicken Scratch. It's a matter of honor."

"Good luck," Eve said. She was from Texas, and a Texan fought till the bloody end.

"Would you like a drink?"

"Not until we're finished with the game," Eve said.

Chapter Three

After consuming a gourmet meal, Eve and the Deveraux clan engaged in a death match of Chicken Scratch. They cajoled her into playing more than two games and each of them won once, but Eve won most overall, much to the siblings' dismay. Stefan had been forced to leave early to take a call.

Jacques bared his teeth playfully. "You're in our targets now even more than ever. Don't get used to winning."

"I'll try not to," Eve drawled, "but since most of my experience is with winning…" She gave a mock shrug.

Phillipa giggled. "She pummeled us even after all our practice."

Eve smiled. "You have to remember that I've been playing this game practically since the cradle."

"That's okay," Bridget said, putting her nose in the

air. "We're just getting started. We *will* conquer Chicken Scratch *and* you."

"Well, you'll have to do it without me for a while since I'm returning to university," Jacques said.

Bridget rose and gave her brother a big hug around his neck, which seemed to surprise him. "I'll miss you. Just be careful with the girls. You know how Stefan is about living down the Deveraux playboy image."

"I'm careful, but I'll never lock myself away from the women the way Stefan does."

"Yes, well, that may be part of the reason he's always in a bad mood. I may put together a plan to change things in that area," Bridget said, her eyes glinting with a diabolical gleam.

Eve almost felt sorry for Stefan. "Time for me to go. Thank you again for the wonderful dinner and company. Good luck at university, Jacques."

"Thank you," Jacques said, rising. "I'll look forward to a rematch when I return on break."

"My pleasure, Your Highness," she said, then looked at Bridget and Phillipa. "Sweet dreams."

"And to you," Phillipa said, smiling.

Eve left the palace and headed for the staff quarters, when she overheard a muttered string of oaths followed by a succession of what she suspected were more expletives in a language she didn't understand coming from behind a tall hedge. What she did understand was that Stefan was the one voicing the litany. For a millisecond, she considered continuing down her path away from him, but some part of her wouldn't allow it.

Turning around, she took in a breath of the night air filled with the scent of flowers, and then peeked through a large hedge. Stefan stood with his back to her, hands on hips, still hissing in frustration. "I hope it's not the landscaping that has you so upset," she said. "If that's true, then your groundskeepers better grab a canoe and get off the island."

Silence followed, then a heavy sigh. He turned toward her voice and his gaze found her immediately. "Join me," he said. "If you dare."

For a moment, she wondered if she really did dare. Then she shook off the silly thought. Sure he was a prince, but he was still just a man. She walked through the maze of hedging to step inside the small courtyard. "Needed some fresh air, eh?" she asked. "What's got you so pissed off this time?"

"This time," he said, lifting a dark brow of disapproval. "The way you say that suggests I'm pissed off most of the time."

"If the shoe fits," she said. "You stayed upset with Tina for a long time."

"She abandoned ship with zero notice," he pointed out.

"True, but pregnancy trumps charity teas," she countered. "And when are you not frustrated with Bridget?"

"Tell me the truth," he said, dipping his head close to hers. "Would you want her for your employee?"

He made an excellent point, but she didn't want to contribute to the strife-ridden relationship between the two of them. "I don't think Bridget is the reason you were swearing at the shrubbery a few moments ago."

He held her gaze for a long moment and sighed. "That's correct," he said, then turned away, shoving his hands into his pockets.

"Just curious," she said. "What language were you using?"

"Italian, French and Greek," he said with a shrug.

"Must be something big to require swearing in four languages," she said.

He stood with his back to her for a long moment and she wondered if it might be best if she left. She didn't appear to be helping.

"For some time, I've been trying to recruit a new medical specialist for Chantaine's health care. Our current chief of health and medicine is retiring soon and we need to bring in a younger M.D. for this position. I'd all but sealed the deal when the doctor of choice announced he'd chosen another position."

Surprise rushed through her. "Wow, you have your finger in a lot of pies. I didn't know you were involved in health care. I figured someone else was in charge of that."

"There have been other people in charge of Chantaine's health care, but I'm taking a more active role than my predecessors. It's not acceptable to me to coast when my family has received such an enormous benefit from our birthright. It's time for us to give in return. Some in the government welcome my input and some do not."

The passion in his voice emanated throughout the space they shared. "I don't know what the position of ruling prince entails, but I had thought it was more about decorum than governing."

"I've been extensively educated in matters of government, world economics, health care policy and infrastructure design. I'm not going to let all that go to waste by sitting on a yacht in the Aegean Sea and showing up for photo ops every couple of months."

"Okay," she said warily. It was obvious this was a touchy subject. "I wasn't suggesting you spend your life on yacht, although it may not be a bad idea for a vacation every now and then. You seem pretty wound up. Maybe you *should* take a little vacation."

He met her gaze and his lips twitched. "How many vacations have you taken?"

"I wasn't born into your world. My family was very poor," she said. "I worked as a matter of survival, through high school, then paid for most of my own college education. As soon as I finished, I worked that job until I came here. There's been no time for vacation."

"But even if there were, I suspect you wouldn't take it. You had to be forced to spend a day at the beach today. You and I are alike. We don't want to take a break until the job is done."

"Yes, but your job will never be done," she said. "If you don't pace yourself, you're going to burn out everyone around you, including yourself."

"You sound almost as if you care," he said.

His response took her off guard. "Maybe I shouldn't, but I guess I do," she said, surprised at how much she was beginning to care for the whole Devereaux family, including Stefan. Unnerved, she decided to leave. "Well, since I don't think I'm helping you get to your royal Zen state, I'll head to my room—"

He reached out to wrap his hand around her wrist. "Au contraire, you underestimate yourself."

Her heart jumped at the sensation of his thumb skimming the underside of her wrist. "I have enormous confidence," she said more breathlessly than she'd intended, "that I have very little effect on you except to irritate you."

His eyes darkened with a hint of challenge that made her a little nervous. "Again," he said, tugging her closer. "You underestimate yourself. You make me curious."

He lifted one of his fingers to her lips, and she felt a

buzzing sensation that started at her mouth and seemed to travel down every nerve ending in her body. "No need to be curious," she said, wondering why her lungs weren't functioning properly. "I'm boring."

He gave a low laugh and shook his head. "No chance. I think you may be a little curious about me."

She opened her mouth to protest, but the lie stuck in her throat. The truth was she found Stefan much more fascinating than she'd expected. He leaned closer and closer, and she held her breath in a mix of expectation and—strangely—fear. She would have to figure out the latter. Why on earth should she be afraid of—

His mouth took hers and every thought except him left her. His lips felt smooth and sensual. There was a reason she should hold back, but she couldn't quite muster it from her cloudy mind. His tongue teased the seam of her lips and she instinctively opened, wanting more. Something inside her cut loose and she arched against him, craving the sensation of his hard chest against her breasts.

She lifted her hands, sinking her fingers into the hair at the nape of his neck. It was surprisingly soft while the rest of him was oh, so hard. In an instant, the tenor of the kiss changed from exploring to hot and aching. She felt his hand slide to the back of her hips, pulling her against him intimately.

Her heart hammered in her chest, her blood roared through her veins like wildfire. She felt an indelible connection that seemed to go deeper than her cells. Crazy, some part of her said, but it was faint compared to the desire, need or whatever it was that filled her to bursting.

He gave a low groan that vibrated deliciously through her. The need inside her grew exponentially.

"I must have you," he muttered against her mouth. He swore. "I want you here, now," he said and took her mouth in another, more passionate, less controlled kiss.

She craved more of his passion, less of his control. Some part of her trusted him like she'd never trusted any other man.

Groaning again, he pulled his mouth from hers and tucked her head beneath his chin. The sound of their breaths mingled with a bird calling in the distance. Eve's mind spun like a water spout. Even though she knew she would drown, she didn't want it to stop.

"I'll figure this out," he said in a low voice. "We'll have an arrangement. We can meet in secret. I'll call you and give you a key to—"

"Arrangement," she echoed, her mind starting to function again. "Secret?" She looked up at him. "What are you talking about?"

"Surely, you don't expect a public relationship with me."

She blinked, not sure what she'd expected.

He gently squeezed her shoulders. "Eve, neither you nor I want to carry out an affair in public."

Affair. It just sounded dirty. Icky.

"Do you really want the press investigating every bit of your past? Every bit of your family's past? Do you want to endure the speculation of being a prospective princess of Chantaine?"

"Princess?" she finally was able to say. "I have never, nor will I ever be, a princess in any sense of the word."

"Exactly," he said and chuckled. Then he turned serious and laced his fingers through hers. "Does that mean you and I should deprive ourselves?"

His touch almost short-circuited her brain function. She frowned as she tried to concentrate. She closed her eyes and tried to think. His scent slid past her self-defenses. She frowned. "I don't know about this. I'm going to have to think about it."

Silence followed. "Excuse me. You're going to have to think about it?"

Eve opened her eyes and nodded. "Yes. You're not just my boss, you're a prince, for Pete's sake. This could turn into one big, hot mess."

"You're refusing my suggestion because I'm a prince?" he said more than asked, and he didn't sound particularly pleased.

She shrugged. "Well, yes. It's not as if a relationship between you and me could go anywhere. Obviously, you agree it's a dead-end adventure. And if you fell in love with me, it would be terribly messy."

He stared at her in amazement. "If I fell in love with you?"

She nodded. "It has happened before."

"I suppose it didn't occur to you that you could fall in love with me," he said in a lethally sexy voice.

She swallowed over a knot of denial. "It's not likely," she said.

He tilted his head to one side. "Why is that, *chérie?*"

Her nerve endings were still leap-frogging over themselves, but she refused to give in to the situation. "Because I've never fallen in love before. Why on earth would I start with you?"

He blinked as if he hadn't heard her correctly.

"Well, other than the fact that you're sexy, intelligent and probably loaded," she said and felt as if she were digging herself deeper into a hole. She didn't like the quicksand sensation at all. Eve preferred staying in control and that was what she would do right now. "I think we should just forget this ever happened."

He laughed, which infuriated her. "Do you think you can do that? Do you think it will be that easy?"

"We're both adults," she said, pushing aside her doubts. "I've had to exercise mind over matter many times during my life. I'm sure you have, too. There," she said, extending her hand. "Let's shake on it."

He took her hand, but instead of shaking it, he shook his head. Then he lifted her hand and turned it so her wrist was open and vulnerable. He pressed his mouth against her skin, and she felt her pulse jump. "Sorry, Eve, I don't make promises I don't intend to keep."

Eve successfully avoided Stefan for the next three days. She told herself that if she created some distance between herself and the kiss that had somehow turned into an *event,* then she would gain the proper perspective, which was that it had been just a kiss and the reason she'd experienced all those feelings was because she'd been tired. Most important, she felt more in control when she wasn't around Stefan.

The day before the parade, she was checking off the items on her countdown list. She couldn't deny a bit of nerves in anticipation of the event, but was satisfied she'd done as much preparation as possible during the time she'd been in Chantaine. She'd touched base with all the riders except for Count Christo. The man had completely ignored her calls. He was the one who liked to wield a whip, and she was determined to find a way to extract it from him before he mounted one of her darlings.

She picked up the phone to call the groomer, when

she heard a knock on her door. Glancing up, she found Phillipa in the doorway. "Well, hello, Your Highness. What brings you here?"

Plastering a smile on her face, Phillipa laced her fingers together, then unlaced them. "Please call me Phillipa. This is just a little visit. I know the big day is tomorrow and I wanted to see how you're doing."

Eve noticed that the bookish princess shifted from one foot to the other. "Is something wrong?"

"Oh, what could be wrong?" Phillipa asked, walking into the small office. "Have you been here all day? Did you go out for lunch?"

Confused, Eve wondered what was behind Phillipa's discomfort. "We've been grooming today, so I've been here since 6:00 a.m. I ate a sandwich at my desk for lunch. Are you sure there's nothing bothering you? Are *you* concerned about the parade tomorrow?"

Phillipa waved her hand dismissively. "Oh, no. People don't focus on me. I know how to keep a low profile."

"Okay," Eve said, still confused by the visit. "Is there something I can do for you?"

Phillipa shrugged and smiled again a bit too brightly. "Not a thing. Stefan and Bridget both have events today, so they asked me to stop in and visit you."

"That was nice," Eve said, torn between the royals' compassion and her desire for them to have complete confidence in her. "I've hammered out all the details."

Phillipa clasped her hands together. "What are your plans for the rest of the day?"

"Double check my to-do list for tomorrow, give the beauties a little extra attention, then hit the sack," she said. "Why?"

"Just curious. I can have chef deliver a light dinner to your quarters," she said.

"Not necessary. I won't be eating much anyway."

"Oh, I insist," Phillipa said. "All of us are very pleased with the job you're doing. We're very happy that you're here in Chantaine."

"Thank you," she said, wishing she could feel more pleased, but something just didn't ring right about this situation. Although Phillipa had been warm and friendly to Eve, she'd never visited her in the stables. Eve had been told the youngest princess was working a grueling schedule to complete her advanced degree as quickly as possible.

"You're welcome. I look forward to seeing you tomorrow," Phillipa said and turned away.

Eve frowned for a moment. Something was going on, but she wasn't sure what it was. She groaned in frustration. Maybe she was just being paranoid.

After a restless night, Eve arose when it was dark and dressed in a formal riding outfit. She much preferred to stay in the background but had been told that the press might ask her a few questions. After eating a protein bar and drinking a cup of coffee, she went to the stables and supervised the rest of the grooming. The parade was scheduled for two o'clock and would depart from the Palace Square.

One of her missions was to separate Count Christo from his famed whip. The elderly man strutted around his assigned horse. Eve had assigned the man Pilar, a lovely older mare. "She's beautiful, isn't she?" Eve said to the count. "Pardon me, I'm Eve Jackson, the royal stable master. I've heard of you. Aren't you the famous Count Christo?"

The count lifted his shoulders and chin in a show of pride. "Yes, I am, and yes, this is a lovely mare. Are you sure she'll be able to keep up with me? I'm quite the horseman, you know," he said, pulling out his whip and tapping it against his hand.

Eve's stomach dipped at the sight of the whip. "Pilar has one of the best pedigrees in the prince's stable. She has spirit and she responds well to a gentle lead. I'm sure you've encountered that kind of mount before."

"Of course," he said, still tapping his hand with the whip.

"Would you mind if I looked at your whip? I've never seen one quite like that before," she said.

"It's been passed down through generations of my family. Napoleon gave it to one of my great-uncles," he said as he handed it to her.

"It looks as if it's barely been used at all," she said, sliding her fingers over the leather.

"Oh, of course not," the count said. "It's mostly for show. A true horseman only uses a whip in the direst circumstance."

A sliver of relief slid through her and she smiled. "You're a wise man."

"You were worried I would whip the horse," he mused, surprising her with his perception.

"It's my job to be protective of them and anyone who rides them," she said.

His lips lifted in a half smile. "Don't worry. The whip shall remain sheathed."

She sighed and dipped her head. "Thank you very much, Count Christo."

"My pleasure," the count said. "It's nice to see the prince's new stable master so conscientious. A refreshing change."

"Thank you again," she said, this time unable to resist

a smile, then left to check on the other riders and horses. She came upon Bridget on one of the geldings.

"Everything okay?" Eve asked, automatically checking the security of the saddle and stirrups.

"Peachy, as you Yanks would say," Bridget said. "The good news is that Stefan found a way to take care of those pesky protesters."

Eve blinked. "Protesters?" she echoed in confusion.

Bridget grimaced. "Oh, no. Stefan's assistant didn't call you? We thought he would be the best one to explain the problem."

"What problem?" Eve demanded, her mind whirling at all the problems protesters could cause. What if they decided to throw rocks at the riders or horses? She shuddered at the thought.

"There was an article in the newspaper yesterday. Stefan and I were busy, so we sent Phillipa around to check on you until Stefan's assistant got in touch with you. I can't believe he didn't do that," Bridget said with a frown. "I assure you Stefan will be furious. But he's fixed it. The royal guard will march alongside the parade to protect us."

Eve frowned. This was supposed to be a joyous occasion. A celebration of Chantaine's beautiful horses. "Why the protest?" she asked.

Bridget sighed. "The citizens think Stefan is spending too much money on the horses…and his new horse master. To them, the horses don't earn their keep."

"Well, that would be easily fixed," Eve said.

"How?" Bridget asked.

"Put Black out to stud. The payment for his sperm could feed a third-world country. Sounds like it's time to spread it around," she said.

Bridget snickered. "Can't wait to see you convince Stefan of that."

Furious that he hadn't discussed this with her, she balled her fists, but hid them behind her back. "No time like the present. Later, Your Highness."

Eve searched the crowd for His Highness and immediately spotted him. He stood tall and confident, resplendent in his dress riding clothes next to Black. She marched toward him.

"Your Royal Highness," she said and bent her knees. As a curtsy, it sucked big-time, but it was better than nothing.

"Ms. Jackson. Good to see you. All the horses are in good form," he said.

She moved closer. "I just hope they *remain* in good form. The *protest* I never heard about could cause problems."

"I've taken care of it," he said.

"I should have been informed. It will look ridiculous to have an army of soldiers escorting the horses. This is supposed to a celebration of pride in the heritage of the royal stables of Chantaine."

"Unfortunately, not all the citizens see it that way," he said.

"There's an easy solution to the money problem," she said.

"What's that?" he asked, glancing around the crowd.

"Release Black's seed," she said.

His head whipped around as he focused on her. "Pardon me?"

"You know what I'm saying. You need to let Black provide stud service. You'll make tons of money."

"I've been waiting—"

"For what? The perfect filly?" she asked.

His eyebrows knitted in disapproval. "Who are you to tell me when I should send my stallion out for stud?"

"I am the royal stable master. You hired me for this very purpose," she said, lifting her chin.

A trumpet sounded. "We'll discuss this later."

"Darn right, we will," she said. "And you better cut the number of guards for this party in half or you're going to look like you're headed into war."

Chapter Four

Eve walked the route of the parade next to the horses. Actually, she ran, trotted, skipped and walked, dividing her attention between the horses and potential protesters. At one turn in the street, she heard hecklers and searched the crowd. Within seconds, the palace guard swarmed like bees. She wished she could talk to them and tell them the value of the prized horses that represented their country, but she knew it wasn't her place.

Pushing aside the effects of the heat of the afternoon, she returned to the last of the parade where Stefan rode astride Black. At every turn, the crowd screamed and clapped in delight. Understandably so. Both Stefan and Black were prime specimens. The spectators threw flowers at them, and she was relieved to see Black take it all in stride.

Suddenly from the corner of her eye, she saw a child streak out of the crowd toward Stefan and Black.

Instinctively, she chased after the boy child. She barely caught him in her arms.

"Prince Stefan," the child wailed. "I want to ride with Prince Stefan."

"Sorry, sweetie," she said as the child struggled in her arms. "I don't want you to get caught in the horse's legs. I don't want you to get hurt."

She felt Stefan's glance at her and looked up at him. Her gaze met his, and the connection between them zinged again. He glanced at the boy and lifted his hand, waving her to bring the child to him.

"Are you sure?" she called, surprised yet not.

He nodded and she carried the little boy to him. One of the guards stepped forward to help lift the boy into the saddle in front of Stefan. The crowd roared with delight. "Find his parents to meet me at the end of the route."

Eve searched the crowd and immediately spotted the astonished, beaming parents of the boy. The young couple were already walking down the street. The father carried a sleeping infant in an infant carrier on his back.

Eve caught up with them. "Hello, I'm Eve Jackson, the royal horse master. Is that your son taking a ride with Prince Stefan?"

The woman gave a huge nod, clearly still stunned. "My son, Ricardo, he is so active. He got away from both my husband and me. Thank you for catching him. I can't believe he is riding with Prince Stefan."

Eve couldn't help smiling at the joy on the couples' faces. "His Royal Highness asked that I make sure you meet your son at the end of the parade. We don't want your son to be frightened."

"Frightened," the father echoed. "I can only wish. The boy shows no fear."

"I understand," she said sympathetically. "Mr.—?"

"Benito," he said. "Raul and Gina Benito, thank you for your kindness."

"My pleasure," she said and gestured for a guard to escort the young couple through the throng of observers. She ran ahead to make sure her assistants were taking care of the horses and riders properly. She knew there would be hundreds of photographs taken by the press of all the horses and riders.

The next hour passed in a flurry of activity as the horses were released from their royal duties and guided back to the barns.

"Ms. Jackson," a man called from a few feet away. "Welcome to Chantaine. Your first royal parade is a huge success."

"Thank you. I'm thrilled for the citizens of Chantaine to get the opportunity to see the beautiful horses that represent their country," she said and motioned to one of her assistants to take two more of the horses back to the stable.

"Oh, but they are not Chantaine's horses. Everyone knows Prince Stefan has a weakness for fine horseflesh. These are Prince Stefan's horses."

"Number one, I wouldn't call it a weakness. Number two, these horses do represent Chantaine just as your beautiful beaches and the palace and palace grounds do."

The man lifted his eyebrow. "Easy for you to say. You make a much better salary than most of the citizens of Chantaine. The prince's horses aren't remotely self-sustaining."

"It wouldn't be hard for them to be self-sustaining," she couldn't keep from saying in defense of the stable.

"What do you mean?"

"Black. He's worth a fortune as a sire," she said, then feared she'd revealed too much. He didn't look like a member of the press and she didn't see a camera. "I need to go. I was taught to earn my keep," she added meaningfully, and then walked away.

Much later that evening after she'd showered and put on her pj's, her cell phone sounded, signaling a text message. She glanced up from the book she was reading and glanced at her phone. Meet me in the lower courtyard in thirty minutes. SD

Eve was torn between irritation and curiosity. The man was way too accustomed to giving orders. In other circumstances, she would have laughed and said forget it. But this was Stefan and the situation was totally different. Plus she was dying of curiosity.

She jumped out of bed and changed into a pair of jeans and a white button-down shirt. With her hair still damp from the shower she'd taken earlier, she just decided to let it air-dry. After a few moments of feeling antsy, she gave in to her restlessness and decided to take the long way to the lower courtyard. She stopped by a bush of blue flowers that reminded her of Texas bluebells and felt a twist of homesickness. Back home, she'd stayed busy with her job, working with the horses on the ranch where her aunt worked and volunteering. Staying busy kept her from thinking too much about how much she missed her brother since he'd left all those years ago. It also kept her from getting involved in a serious relationship. From a young age, Eve had been determined to steer her own ship, and she'd never met a man with whom she'd willingly share the wheel.

She heard the snap of a twig, but before she could turn around she heard his voice.

"Congratulations, Eve. Well done."

Pleasure welled up inside her and she turned around to find Stefan, his shirt partly unbuttoned, his hair mussed and carrying a bottle of champagne and two glasses. Surprised by his gesture, she felt a secret rush of delight. "Congratulations to you, too. The crowd loved it when you gave Ricardo a ride on Black. Champagne?"

He shrugged. "You worked hard. I thought you deserved to celebrate."

"You could have just sent the bottle to my apartment, couldn't you?" she asked, unable to resist the chance to tease him.

He shot her a look with a glint of the devil in his eyes. "Okay, *I* deserve to celebrate, too. Come on," he said and walked toward the lower courtyard. They entered the area surrounded by tall hedges and he gestured toward the stone bench. "Hold these, please," he said and handed her the glasses.

"Wow," she said.

"What?" he asked as he released the cork without spilling a drop. He tilted the liquid into the two glasses.

"You said *please*. I don't hear that word from you all that often," she said and offered him a glass.

"Are you always this charming when someone tries to thank you?"

"You knew what you were getting when you hired me," she said and lifted her glass in salute. "Congratulations on choosing such spectacular horses for your stable and for giving a little boy and his parents the story of their lives."

"Congratulations for pulling it all together," he said and clicked his glass against hers.

They both took a sip of the champagne. "I must confess I was worried about the combination of the protestors and your royal cavalry."

He smothered a chuckle. "Royal *guard*."

"Close enough," she said and took another sip. "Have you been busy with interviews with the press?"

"And a cocktail party with the riders. I told my assistant to make sure you were invited."

She shook her head. "I thought it would be better for me to make sure the real stars were taken care of after the show."

"Of course," he said. "Next time, remember you have staff for that."

"No one refuses the prince?" she said. "Except for his family."

"Are you saying you don't want to attend a party at the palace as a guest?"

She opened her mouth, then closed it. "It's a little out of my everyday routine," she confessed.

"I can't believe you would be intimidated. I haven't seen anything else intimidate you," he said.

"When I was eight years old, my brother told me to never let them see me sweat."

"That's pretty young for that kind of instruction. What was the occasion?" he asked.

Another move due to her parents' inability to keep jobs and pay bills. Another new school when she'd wondered how long they would stay in this place. How long until people found out her father drank away most of his paycheck? "One of those times in elementary school when the kids teased or bullied. It happens to most kids at one time or another."

He looked at her for a long moment and frowned. "I don't like the idea of that."

"What?" she asked, his intent gaze making her stomach slip and slide.

"The idea of someone bullying you."

Something in the way he looked at her made her feel as if she were taking a free fall with no net. She tried to shake it off, but wasn't completely successful. She wasn't accustomed to someone being protective of her. "It didn't happen often," she drawled.

He chuckled. "I bet it didn't," he said and chucked her chin with his index finger. "Do you see him often? Your brother?"

His question slid under her radar, right through her ribs. She rarely mentioned her brother because his absence from her life was still painful to her. "Eli left a long time ago. He had to go. It was the only way." She took a quick breath and shook her head, hating the fact that Stefan had found her vulnerable spot. "Can we talk about something else?"

He paused a half beat, then nodded. "Of course. We're here to celebrate," he said with his most charming smile and clicked his glass against hers again.

She took a quick sip but spilled the champagne on the front of her shirt as she pulled the glass away. Frustration prickled through her. "This is why I don't drink very often," she muttered, futilely pulling at her shirt.

"I can see where it would be distracting during a date," Stefan said.

Glancing up, she saw his gaze fixed on her breasts. She looked down and was mortified by the outline of her nipples against the shirt. "Oh, great. This is embarrassing," she said and crossed her arms over her breasts. "See why I'm not big on formal parties? Even a private celebration in the seclusion of a faraway court-yard is not safe."

Stefan took her glass and tossed it onto the soft bed of grass along with his, then took her chin in his fin-gers. "Trust me, Eve. If a man chooses to be with you in a courtyard, he's not thinking of safety," he said and lowered his mouth to hers.

Her heart stuttered in her chest. In another lifetime, she wondered if she could have turned him away. She'd turned so many others away. But she sensed that Stefan was strong enough. Man enough. She paused a heart-beat, then opened her mouth, opened herself to him.

Something between them clicked and snapped at the same time. If she believed in that kind of thing, she would have said it was electrical. But Eve didn't believe. At least, she never had before.

He deepened the kiss, sliding his tongue past her lips, tasting and testing her. She slid her hands upward to his strong shoulders, wanting to absorb his strength and power into her. The kiss turned deeply passionate, almost carnal, making her cling to him.

He murmured something delicious against her lips, and suddenly she felt the night air against her back as he unbuttoned the bottom of her shirt. His hand on the bare skin of her waist stopped her breath. Seconds later, one of his hands slid upward to her breast, and she pushed against it, resenting the barriers of her shirt and bra. She wanted to feel his skin.

Part of her was shocked at the force of her desire, but another part of her knew she'd been waiting for this—for him—for years. She felt as if she were riding a tsunami of sensation and refused to fight it. She tugged at his shirt, he pulled at hers, and buttons flung loose. Seconds later, he unfastened her bra and her breasts sprang free. He immediately covered one of her breasts with his hand.

Her nipple was hard and sensitized to his touch. He swore under his breath as he toyed with her nipple at the same time as he French-kissed her. She drank in the spicy, masculine scent of him and felt as if the world was turning sideways.

Stefan clasped his hand beneath her hips and lifted her upward. At the same time, he lowered his head to take her nipple into his mouth, she felt his hardness pressed against her.

Dizzy with want, she slumped against him.

Stefan groaned, lifting his head and pulling her tightly against him. "We need to be together," he whispered. "I want you in my bed."

A shiver of the need he expressed raced through her. "How? Where?"

He gave a rough sound of frustration. "If it were up to me, it would be here and now. But I want privacy for the both of us."

She sighed and tried to gather her wits. Was this what she really wanted? Was he what he really wanted? Eve was only certain of one thing. She couldn't *miss* him. Stefan affected her in a way no man ever had, and she craved the ultimate closeness with him. She wanted him so much it scared her, but she wasn't going to let her fear keep her from him.

"Then when?" she finally asked and met his gaze.

His dark eyes met hers, and she saw the strained passion there. The strength of it reassured her rather than frightened her. "You make it difficult for me not to take you now, *chérie*. Tomorrow night," he said. "I'll make arrangements for you to come to my suite. I'll work it out tomorrow."

A ripple of anticipation and nerves raced through her. "It may not be wise—"

He covered her lips with his fingers. "It's beyond choice. We both feel it."

She nodded, savoring the heat of his body. "Okay," she said, then whispered, "But this is totally against all my rules."

He chuckled and lifted her hand to his lips. "Mine, too, Eve. Mine, too. Now, before I give into my darker urges, I'd better walk you back to your quarters."

"What about the champagne and the glasses?" she asked.

"Don't worry. I'll send a member of my security to collect them," he said and took her hand. "Let's go."

The next morning, she awakened a little later than usual. Stefan had insisted she take a day of vacation. So she slept until 9:00 a.m. This was the first morning she'd woken up not feeling like she was going to hyperventilate. Not that she would admit that to a soul.

Stretching her arms, she yawned, then smiled, pleased that the parade had gone off without a hitch. She'd passed her first test. Thank goodness. A sliver of anxiety rippled through her at the thought of Stefan's plans for tonight. Had she lost her mind? He was not only her boss, he was a prince.

He was also a man, she told herself. A man she wanted and who wanted her. Taking a deep breath, she slid out of her bed and stepped onto the carpet. Her toes appreciated the soft cushion for her first steps of the day. She realized she'd hit the ground running so much she hadn't noticed the small comfort.

Stretching again, she walked to the tiny kitchenette and started her coffee. She peeked inside her mostly bare refrigerator and pulled out cream for her coffee, marmalade for her toast and orange juice. She popped bread in the toaster and wandered toward the door of her quarters to pick up the paper. She'd made double sure she would receive the daily paper. After the incident with the protestors, she'd decided she needed to stay informed even though the Chantaine newspaper read like an odd combination of a scandal sheet and traditional news.

The front page was filled with photographs of the parade, featuring the royal family and government officials on horseback. The largest photo showed Stefan riding with the young boy on Black. Her heart twisted at the image of him. Lord help her, the man was so handsome. She noticed the way his hand curled around the boy, holding him securely. The boy smiled broadly while Stefan's mouth lifted in a ghost of a smile.

Fascinating man, she thought. For a moment she wondered what Stefan would be like if he weren't a prince. She closed her eyes, trying to imagine him as a Texan. He would be a Renaissance man, she decided, with a huge empire. Obscenely successful, she thought. Nothing less would be acceptable. His woman would be… She frowned in concentration. Blonde, beautiful, but brainy. The perfect accessory on his arm.

Nothing like me.

She frowned again, feeling a stab of displeasure and immediately pushing it aside. She shook her head at herself. This was what happened when she had time on her hands. Her mind traveled down all kinds of crazy paths. She rattled the paper and refocused, scanning the rest of the front page. A headline at the bottom of the page grabbed her attention. Royal Stable Master Reports Prince's Horse Is Worth Billions for Sperm.

Billions! She'd never said billions. Who was reporting this? She hadn't talked to anyone...except the man at the end of the parade. Her stomach sank in realization. Even though she'd cut the conversation short, she'd obviously said more than she should.

Less than a moment later, her cell phone rang. She darted through the living area to her bedside table where she'd left it and immediately glanced at the caller ID. Her stomach sank even further. The palace office was calling.

"Hello. Eve Jackson," she said and began to pace.

"Ms. Jackson, this is Louis calling for Franz Cyncad. We have a public relations concern. Your presence is required in the Palace Office."

Great, she thought. Franz was right up there at the top of the food chain. "I can be there in twenty minutes."

"Mr. Cyncad is finalizing the appropriate strategy. He will meet with you after lunch at fourteen hundred."

Eve bit back an oath. Not only did she know she would be disciplined or perhaps even fired, now she had to *wait* to hear about it. "I'll be there."

"Very well. Goodbye," he said and disconnected the call.

Adrenaline pumping through her, Eve immediately went into survivor mode. With her upbringing, it was second nature. She wondered if she should go ahead and make a call to her former boss. She'd made sure to leave on good terms. She might not be able to get her exact position, but the company had been pleased with her work. Or she could start contracting for several horse ranchers. Stefan would pay her severance.

Her heart was hammering and her stomach was

twisting as she glanced out her window at the cobblestone drive, the lush green trees and pink flowers. She felt a deep sense of regret twist through her. For the first time in weeks, she was acutely aware of the fact that she didn't want to leave. She loved the horses, and her feelings for Stefan…were overwhelming. Until now, she'd been totally absorbed with the parade and intermittent bouts of homesickness she'd pushed aside. Eve had learned at a very young age that denial was an important tool of survival.

But this wasn't her childhood, and she wasn't going to be chased out of her home due to bankruptcy. So maybe she shouldn't jump off the first available cliff. She took a deep breath and slowly released it.

If she was going to be fired, how did she want to spend her remaining hours on Chantaine?

Stefan? Impossible. Tonight, the night they would have made love, was never going to happen.

She swallowed over a hard lump in her throat. Pushing that option aside, she made her plans. The horses, then the beach.

Eve took a micro-shower, French-braided her hair, then visited the royal beauties in the barn and petted and cooed over them. Her heart twisted at the way they all seemed to know her. Even Black indulged her for a few moments before he stamped away.

She stood for a long moment, inhaling the scent of fresh hay and clean horses, branding it into her memory. Then she grabbed a taxi for the beach and made the driver promise to return to fetch her at twelve forty-five. Eve spread her towel on the sand, stripped down to her bikini and sat down on the beach.

She stared at the waves. Whitecaps topped azure water as the tide crashed into shore. The surf was a little rough. She would test it in a few moments, she decided. For the moment, she would focus on the sensation of sun shining on her and the way the ocean looked as if diamonds flickered on top of it.

Inhaling the unique scent of Chantaine, she tried to find a way to preserve the vanilla beachy smell in her mind, the memory of that evening ride with Stefan. All that would never happen between them flashed through her mind. Eve couldn't stand it. She picked up her towel and scrambled up the sandy hill to the road to hail a taxi.

An hour later, Eve sat in Franz Cyncad's office trying to look cool as she resisted the urge to drum her fingers on her black pants–clad leg. Franz was frowning. Not a good sign. He glanced up at her from behind his desk and his gold-rimmed glasses. "You spoke to Marco LaChalle yesterday during the parade," he finally said.

"I didn't meet anyone named Marco. I was focused on the horses and our surprise child rider. A man approached me toward the end of the parade. I barely spoke to him."

Franz pulled off his glasses. "You told him Black could earn billions in stud fees."

"I told him Black could earn a fortune in stud fees," she corrected, still determined to remain calm.

"He apparently interpreted a fortune as a billion," Franz said.

"That was his interpretation, not mine," she said, now barely resisting the urge to fidget. Was she going to survive this or not? Based on Franz's dour expression, she suspected not.

"Unfortunately, we must deal with Mr. LaChalle's report. We need you to recant your position."

It took a full moment for Franz's comment to sink in. "I can't do that. It would be an outright lie," she said at the same time Stefan walked through the door. "Black *is* worth a fortune in stud fees."

"He's not ready," Stefan said.

"Your Highness," Franz said and stood.

Suddenly, Eve remembered she was supposed to do the curtsy thing. "Yes, Your Highness," she said and stood. "But I disagree. As a professional," she added. "It's appropriate to have a specialist assess a stallion for stud purposes at the age of four. Black is over four. His pedigree is phenomenal. He has the potential to produce amazing foals."

Stefan shot her a cool glance. "You are not the appropriate person to assess when Black should breed."

She nodded in agreement. "True. I'm only the stable master you hired to train and advise you on your horses. So, whatever."

Stefan blinked. "Whatever?"

"American version of do what you want. I've done what I can do," she said.

His eyes narrowed. "What would you suggest, Ms. Jackson?"

Oooh, she thought. The Ms. Jackson wasn't a good sign. "I suggest you get Black assessed by the veterinarian, then get moving with providing his sperm, at a cost, to superior mares. Spreading his sperm is part of his purpose. I'm sure Black would agree with my assessment," she said wryly.

Stefan lifted an eyebrow and paused. "Put out a press release saying the palace is having Black assessed for stud service. Be prepared for a deluge of calls. Keep records. We'll return calls later," he said.

Silence followed. "Will Ms. Jackson be remaining on as stable master? Or will she be moving on?" Franz asked.

"Ms. Jackson remains," Stefan said and turned and left the room.

Eve stared after him, stunned and uncertain.

Franz glowered at her. "God help us. More records. More return calls. Would it have been so hard to recant your position?"

"Sorry," she said. "But yes."

Franz sighed again. "Double the workload," he muttered.

"It will ultimately be double the money. Black will earn his way and make your job easier. Just give it a little time."

"We don't have a lot of time, Ms. Jackson," Franz said. "Chantaine's economy is in the loo. Our people are suffering."

"I'm sorry to hear that, Mr. Cyncad, but the world economy is struggling. Everyone is suffering. We're all going to need to get creative to find a way to get Chantaine on the high road. I'm on your side."

"Hmm," Franz said, putting his glasses his face and returning his attention to the laptop in front of him.

Eve waited a long moment. "Do you need anything else, Mr. Cyncad?"

"Not now, Ms. Jackson. I shall contact you if I need to. You may proceed with your plans for the day."

Eve paused, still confused. "Thank you," she said. "Have a good day."

Franz gave a short nod, and Eve left the man's office,

still unsure of her status. She hadn't been fired. Still, what about her relationship with Stefan? Would she be meeting him tonight? Or not?

Chapter Five

After her meeting with Franz and Stefan, Eve felt at loose ends. She checked on the horses, but it was a day off for them, too. After the weeks of preparation, the royal horses seemed determined to laze their day away. She did busywork in the barns and returned to her room, but she didn't know what to do with herself.

In the back of her mind, she wondered if Stefan still wanted to be with her, but based on his curt appearance this afternoon, she couldn't imagine her phone ringing. Her cell rang, catching her off guard. Her stomach clenched. Was it Stefan? She glanced at the caller ID and felt a stab of disappointment. It was Bridget.

"Hello," Eve said. "How are you?"

"Bored and irritated. I was supposed to go to dinner tonight with a friend, but she bailed because she's not feeling well. You must come with me," she said, sounding autocratic, then changed her tone. *"Pleeeeeeeeeease."*

Eve laughed despite herself. "Sorry, Bridget, but I don't think I would be very good company tonight."

"Oh, why not? The parade was a huge success. I took a quick glance at the photographs in the newspaper. You should be flying high," she said.

"You obviously didn't read the entire front page. There's been some controversy about breeding Black, and I was called to the woodshed by Franz Cyncad."

"Woodshed?" Bridget echoed. "What woodshed?"

"It's a figure of speech. The woodshed is where you're taken for punishment, a spanking."

Bridget gasped. "Franz struck you? Does Stefan know? This is totally unaccepta—"

"No, no, no," Eve said. "Franz didn't spank me. He's just very unhappy with me."

"Oh, well, Franz is always unhappy. It's in his job description. If you had a meeting with Franz, it's all the more reason you should come out to dinner with me. Put on a dress and I'll have my driver pick you up in an hour."

"Bridget—"

"I'm not taking no for an answer," the princess insisted. "Oh, for goodness' sake, this is getting insulting. Am I such horrid company that you won't join me even when you have nothing else to do?"

Eve sighed, still full of conflicting emotions. "Okay, okay. Thank you for inviting me."

"That's the spirit," Bridget said. "Ta-ta for now."

Although she would far prefer a barbecue place where she could wear jeans and a T-shirt, she couldn't fight the urge to *get out*. She took another quick shower and pulled on a black halter dress. Instead of putting up her hair, she blow-dried and fluffed it. Since she had time, she applied a little makeup, mascara, a little bronzer, lip gloss...

Her cell phone rang. She glanced at it, hoping desperately that it was Stefan. But it wasn't. She picked it up. "Hello. Eve Jackson," she said.

"This is Raoul, Princess Bridget's chauffeur," the man said.

Her heart twisting in disappointment, she took a deep breath. "Thank you. I'll be right down." Grabbing a sweater, she took the stairs down to the limo.

Raoul stepped outside. "Ms. Jackson?" he said as he opened the door to the backseat.

"Thank you," she said and climbed into the limo.

"Welcome," Bridget said, smiling as she held two glasses of champagne, one in each hand. "Girls' night."

Eve remembered last night and the champagne she'd shared with Stefan. She slid into the seat and closed her mind to the memory. She accepted the glass extended to her and clicked hers to Bridget's. "Girls' night," she agreed, determined to forget her rotten meeting with Franz Cyncad and the fact that Stefan was clearly displeased with her.

They went to a restaurant in a swanky section of the capital of Chantaine. Eve felt self-conscious at first because they were seated in the center of the restaurant, but Bridget chatted constantly, distracting her. The princess was clearly happy to be away from the palace.

"Do you want to get married?" Eve asked, after Bridget had stared at a hot guy who passed by them.

Bridget shrugged. "Not too early," she said. "There's danger in marrying too young, and I'm determined to avoid it. No kids until I'm thirty years old. I want to have some fun. What about you?"

"I haven't thought much about marriage. I've always thought I would take care of myself. Safer, that way," she said.

"Hmm," Bridget said. "I could find a man who would take care of me. I just don't want to give up what little freedom I have in exchange for that."

"Same here," Eve said and lifted her water glass in salute to Bridget. She'd switched to water awhile back.

"I'm not ready for the night to end," Bridget said. "I know of a club close by."

"I'm not sure that's a good idea," Eve said.

Bridget pouted. "Why not?"

"I'm not much on clubs," Eve said.

Bridget shook her head. "It will be a good change for you. We'll just stay for a few minutes."

"I'm not sure—"

"Oh, for goodness' sake," Bridget said. "It's just one night and trust me, our clubs are nothing compared to Rome or Milan."

"Never been to clubs in Rome or Milan. Don't really need to go," Eve muttered, but felt as if she were being swept forward by a force of nature. Tonight she would ride it. Tomorrow she would return to her boring self.

Forty-five minutes later, she found herself sitting at the bar while Bridget danced with a friend of a friend of a friend on a crowded dance floor. Her bodyguard, Rodney, stood nearby, shifting from one foot to the other, clearly as uncomfortable with the scene as she was. Because Eve was bored out of her mind, she decided to torture herself and checked her cell for messages. So far, there'd been none. She shouldn't be surprised, she supposed.

She glanced at the phone and saw one missed call

from Stefan. Her heart jumped, skipping several beats. Suddenly a text appeared. Where are you?

With Bridget, she texted back.

Why? Never mind.

Eve frowned. What did that mean? She shook her head. This was insane. She'd never gone crazy for any other man. Why should she start now? Stuffing her phone into her purse, she was determined not to give him another thought. At least, not tonight.

The woman was going to drive him insane, Stefan thought as his chauffeur and two of his security detail drove closer to the bar where his sister and Eve were apparently enjoying Chantaine's nightlife. He ground his teeth at the thought of it.

"I'm sure Rodney's had enough of this unplanned excursion," Stefan said. He'd seen this coming with Bridget. He'd just hoped she grown more mature about accepting her duties and security protocol. "If Princess Bridget protests, escort Ms. Jackson to my limousine."

"If she goes calmly, sir?" Georg asked.

"In that unlikely event," Stefan said drily, "Ms. Jackson can ride with the princess."

Four minutes and forty-five seconds later, his sister burst through the door with the assistance of two security men, screaming at the top of her lungs. Eve walked behind them. "You can't do this. It's my night off. I can do what I want. I could have ditched Rodney, but I didn't. Just wait until I get my hands on Stefan. Just wait—"

Stefan watched as Eve put her hand on Bridget's arm as if she were trying to calm her. Bridget pulled back her arm and continued to scream. His sister would likely be embarrassed tomorrow.

"Open the door and offer Ms. Jackson a ride in peace," Stefan said to his top bodyguard, Franco.

"Yes, sir."

Stefan could tell Eve needed some extra explanation in order to leave his wailing sister with her bodyguard. She slid into the seat across from Stefan and he made a mental note to thank his sister when she decided she was speaking to him again. Eve usually wore jeans, but tonight she wore a dress that revealed her long, shapely legs.

"Your Highness, your sister's gonna be ticked off with you for a long time," Eve drawled.

"She'll get over it when I let her take a vacation to Italy soon," he said. "It's unfortunate that you had to witness her—" He wanted to choose his words carefully.

"Hissy fit?" Eve said. "She's on a short leash and doesn't like it."

"There's good reason for it," he said. "I insist on her safety."

She frowned and studied him. "Have there been threats?"

"Threats? Rarely. Risks, always. It's part of the job," he said. "Does that frighten you?"

She crossed her arms over her chest. "I don't like the idea of any of you being hurt."

"Neither do I," Stefan said. "That's why I have only the best security and that is why Bridget and you shouldn't have been in that club tonight. Bridget knows she's supposed to submit her schedule to security before she goes anywhere. She's in a high-profile position now. She can't take the same kinds of risks she could before. Plus, she put you at risk."

Eve's eyes widened in surprise. "Me? The only risk I was facing was boredom at that club."

"I intend to keep it that way," he said and paused. "Why didn't you wait for me? Did you get cold feet?"

She lifted a dark eyebrow. "Based on our lovely conversation during my meeting with Franz, I didn't know what to expect."

"That was about your slip to the press," he said, dismissing the concern. "You are still my employee. Can you compartmentalize or not?"

She met his gaze for a long moment. "I don't know. I know I was raised to say please and thank you and I prefer being treated the same way, even by royalty. I respond better to an invitation than an order."

Stefan realized he would need to take a step back and frustration nicked at him. He wanted Eve in his bed. He couldn't totally explain it, but something about the woman made him keep turning toward her. It was almost as if she had some sort of magnetic pull on him, which was rubbish.

He supposed he could tell his chauffer to return to the staff quarters at the palace and he and Eve could go their separate ways, but Stefan wasn't willing to give up his time with Eve even if she wouldn't be spending the night in his bed as he'd planned. He pressed a button to talk to the driver. "Send security ahead to my Aunt Zoe's house at Gerando Beach. I'll give her a call to see if she minds me dropping in." He turned to Eve. "Would you like to go to the beach tonight?"

"I don't have a suit with me," she said, but her eyes lit with interest.

"No need for one. We'll be on a balcony of a private home listening to live music and watching the surf. Interested?"

She paused a half beat, then smiled and he felt as if

the sun had come out from behind a cloud. "Yes, that sounds nice."

Aunt Zoe was in Switzerland, but she'd left instructions with her staff that her house was always available to the royal family. After Stefan's security finished securing the seaside home, Eve and Stefan walked inside. The two-story foyer featured large windows, an unusual chandelier of crystal and copper, and a double staircase.

"It's beautiful," she said.

"Yes," Stefan agreed and extended his hand to her. "But upstairs is better." He led the way upstairs and down a hallway to a den with a swirling paddle fan overhead, white cushy-looking furniture, a bar and kitchen.

"Aunt Zoe designed it all. It's a hobby for her. She also has homes in Switzerland, Bellagio and Manhattan," he said.

"Sounds like she's a woman on the move," Eve said. "And very talented."

"You like it?" he asked.

"It's luxurious, but soothing at the same time. I just probably wouldn't go with a white couch. I'd be afraid of getting it dirty." She laughed. "No. I'd definitely get it dirty."

He liked the way she enjoyed the house and saw herself in it with a modification. "It's nice being with a woman who's not so—" He paused. "Overly fashion conscious."

She smiled. "Or prissy."

He smiled in return. "That word didn't occur to me."

"Bet it will now," she said.

He swallowed a chuckle. "You still haven't seen the

best part. Come on," he said and led her through the glass doors to the expansive balcony with two chaise longues, a table with an umbrella, and a view of the hippest beach in Chantaine. The music of an American R&B band rose from just beneath them.

She tilted her head quizzically. "That sounds awfully familiar. Are they a cover band for…" She glanced over the balcony. "Americans? Here in Chantaine?"

He shook his head, amused again. "We have many American visitors every year. Some Americans like it here, Eve."

"Well, of course they do," she said. "I just didn't expect to see one of my favorite R&B bands playing on one of Chantaine's beaches."

"Think about it. You play a lot of cities and concert halls. Then you get a chance to play in paradise, all expenses paid."

"How come you never see these gigs listed on the band website?" she asked.

"Privacy's also one of our charms."

"Hmm. Maybe it shouldn't be," she said.

"What do you mean?" he asked, unable to conceal a trace of indignation. "Part of Chantaine's attraction is that we're not overexposed."

"I hate to bust your ego, but before I met your sister Tina, I didn't know Chantaine existed. Granted, I'm not a world traveler, but I'm college educated and always got As in Geography. If Chantaine's economy is suffering, maybe it's time to let the cat of the bag about what a great place this is."

"It's a delicate balance," he said. "The advisers and state officials can't agree."

"Makes you wish you were the boss of everything," she said and smiled.

"Enough about business. Let's enjoy the music," he said, joining her at the balcony railing.

"And the ocean breeze," she said, lifting her chin and closing her eyes.

He skimmed his hand down the inside of her arm. "And the company. Would you like a drink?"

Her eyes flashed open, and she leaned close to him, and she whispered, "Are you sure we should raid your aunt's liquor cabinet?"

Stefan laughed, full and hard, at the ridiculous question. He hadn't laughed this hard in a long time. The notion that his aunt would be upset at his use of anything in her home was ridiculous. He led Eve inside to the bar. "I'll replace anything we use," he assured her. "What's your pleasure?"

"I'm not a big drinker," she said, looking at the rows of liquor, but stopped when she saw a bottle of bourbon. "But I could sip on a Texas Rose."

"What's that?" he asked.

She gave a mock gasp. "You mean I know something you don't?"

"What's in it?" he asked. "I'll fix it."

"You?" she asked, her eyes rounded in surprise. "I thought you had staff for everything."

"I do, but that doesn't mean I can't do most of what my staff can do," he said. "Why do you think I fired so many stable masters?"

She winced. "That's scary."

"Ingredients," he demanded and stepped behind the bar.

"I've only had it a few times," she said. "Bourbon, orange juice, cherry liquor…and champagne."

He lifted an eyebrow, but grabbed the bourbon from the second shelf. The bottle was dusty. "Prissy drink."

"Maybe," she said. "But if you drink it, too, you can always say you've had a Texas Rose."

Stefan paused as he pulled out a chilled can of orange juice and met her gaze. "I've never needed to embellish my successes."

"There's always a first," she returned and pulled her long bangs behind her ear.

Her ears were naked except for silver studs. It struck him that he would love to see her dripping with Chantaine's royal family's jewels…and nothing else. He felt himself grow hard and ground his teeth. On impulse he mixed two drinks at once, then poured the liquid into two glasses filled with ice. Walking from behind the bar, he gave Eve her glass and lifted his. "To a Texas Rose," he said, "transplanted to Chantaine."

She clicked his glass with hers and took a sip. "Not bad for a prince," she said.

Stefan resisted the urge to seduce her to lie down on one of those white couches and make wild, crazy love with her. "Let's go outside, Madamoiselle Texas Rose," he said and guided her to the balcony again.

They stood at the balcony and she sipped her drink, the wind lifting her hair from her shoulders. Stefan slid his arm around her waist. "You're homesick," he said. "What do you miss most?"

"You weren't supposed to notice," she said, giving a soft smile as she looked at him. "I was trying not to let it show."

"You didn't answer my question. What do you miss most?" he asked.

"The familiarity, my aunt, barbecue. This isn't my turf," she said.

"It will be," he said. "It won't take long. Chantaine is small compared to Texas."

"But complex and still very foreign to me," she said.

"That will change soon enough."

"If you say so," she said.

The doubt in her voice surprised him. She was usually so confident, so ready to come back at him. "What made you question your ability?"

"Today shook me a little," she confessed.

"Franz?" he said and gave a short laugh. "He's a necessary nuisance. This won't be your last run-in with him."

She made a face. "I'd like it to be. I didn't know whether I would be staying or going."

"You're too expensive to let go," he said.

"I feel so much better now," she said in a dry tone.

"You're good at what you do. You're just not accustomed to the way our press works. Just don't talk to them until you learn the ropes."

"Who's going to teach me the ropes? Franz?" she asked with dread in her voice.

"No. My assistant or me. You can always call him," he said. "You can always call me." He couldn't remember when he'd told any other woman such a thing.

The band eased into a slow, sensual tune. Stefan's hands itched to touch her in ways he knew wouldn't happen tonight. "Dance?" he asked, setting down his glass on one of the tables.

Meeting his gaze, she let him take her glass and do the same with his. Then she walked into his arms, and Stefan sighed at the sensation of her body close to his, where she belonged. He drank in the subtle spice and sweet combination of her scent. Her silky hair skimmed his jaw and her breasts brushed against his chest with each movement.

Holding her eased something inside him at the same time he felt need stretch inside him. He tried to ignore the need and focus on how good she felt. For a full moment, the only sounds were of the sultry song, their hushed breaths and in the background, ocean waves rolling into the surf.

"Have you ever had a more perfect moment than this?" she whispered, lifting her mouth just beneath his ear.

He searched his brain and came up empty. "No," he murmured, pulling her even closer.

The song finally faded away, and she lifted her head, searching his eyes. The expression of wanting he saw there made his gut twist. The connection between them was shocking in its intensity. He lowered his head and took her mouth in a kiss. She immediately responded, tasting of oranges, bourbon and something forbidden.

Although he was already aroused, he couldn't resist feeding himself on her mouth. He felt her arms climb around his neck as she kissed him with equal intensity. He slid his own hand to the small of her back, bringing her intimately against him. He wondered if she would pull away. Instead, she wriggled against him. His heart stuttered in his chest.

"You make it difficult for me to show restraint," he muttered against her mouth.

"Is that what I'm supposed to be doing? Helping you show restraint?" she asked, her voice husky, her lips already swollen. She grazed his neck with an almost kiss and another twist of need ricocheted through him, this one stronger than before.

"You need to understand that everything will change once we become lovers," he told her.

"Is this the standard warning required by the

advisers?" she asked, pulling back slightly with a sliver of wry amusement in her eyes.

"No," he said. "It's just me being straight with you."

"Aren't things already different between us?" she asked.

"Yes, but I am determined to be discreet. I don't want you or your reputation to be affected."

"Can we just make this between you and me?" she asked.

"My position makes it difficult," he said.

"I don't want the position. I want the man," she said.

Her words nearly put him over the edge, nearly made him pick her up, lay her down on the couch and take her that moment. He'd spent a lifetime being the prince instead of a man. "You really don't care about my title, do you?"

"To be perfectly honest, Stefan, I'd probably like you more without it," she drawled.

A sliver of exultation rushed through him. "I like your honesty," he said, lifting a strand of her hair. "I like you too much."

Her eyes darkened in awareness. "It's good to know I'm not the only one feeling this way."

"No fear of that," he said in a dry tone and gave in to the urge to sink his hands into her hair and pull her head toward him.

They kissed again and he linked one of his hands with hers.

Eve's heart hadn't beat regularly since she'd first laid eyes on Stefan tonight. She wasn't sure when she would breathe normally again. The world was tilted upside down, the night was spinning and heaven help her, she liked it. She liked the way his mouth moved against hers. The way his body felt against hers. The way his voice felt against her ears and skin…

She wanted to feel more of his skin. More of him. Seeking his lips, she tugged at his shirt, unfastening one button, then two… She spread her hands over his chest and sighed at the indulgent luxury of feeling his muscles beneath her fingertips. He sighed, too, and the sound was more delicious than the most decadent chocolate. The sea air and the sound of the surf only added to the ambiance.

"You have muscles," she said. "When do you *ever* get the chance to work out?"

His laugh rumbled through her. "Every morning at 4:30 a.m."

She winced, still sliding her hands over his bare chest. "That's insane."

"And what time do you get up?"

"Five-thirty," she said. "Compared to you, I'm a slacker." She kissed him again. "But maybe if I had to deal with your advisers, I'd get up at four-thirty to work off some of my frustration to keep from wringing their skinny necks."

He chuckled again. "Some of their necks are fat."

Shaking her head, she sank her face into his bare shoulder and inhaled deeply. "I like the way you smell."

"I'm not wearing cologne," he said and lifted her head. The expression in his eyes was just this side of ravenous. "Eve, you're not acting like a woman who wants me to hold back."

Fighting a flutter of nerves, she licked her suddenly dry lips. Fish or cut bait, she told herself. "Maybe my actions are doing all the real talking."

She felt him slide one of his hands all the way down

her back and he pulled her against his arousal. He made sure she knew just how thoroughly he was aroused. "Are you sure? I want you to be sure."

"Another disclaimer for the advisers?"

He narrowed his eyes. "No. For me."

She took a deep breath. "I'm sure." She smiled. "Ravish me."

He shook his head. "What an invitation," he said and pushed her dress down her shoulders. Three heartbeats later, her bra snapped loose and his mouth covered hers.

Eve knew she was venturing into new territory, but she was determined not to be shy about it. She wanted to feel everything. She wanted to feel bold and in control, but the truth was she felt vulnerable. Eve refused to give in to weakness.

Instead she focused on her senses. She traced her fingers through his crisp hair, down to his strong shoulders and chest. He slid his hands over her bare breasts and she shuddered. Her internal and external temperature rose exponentially. Eve had never been high, but she suspected this was what it might feel like. Her head was spinning, she found it difficult to breathe and a wicked euphoria raced through her veins.

Somehow, during the next kiss, her dress and panties were pooled at her feet. She scrubbed at his arms and felt remnants of his shirt. His pants-clad thigh slid between hers.

"You have on too many clothes," she said, her voice sounding husky to her own ears.

He shook his head. "Once my clothes are gone, my control will follow."

"Thank goodness," she said.

Chapter Six

Her words had the effect of gasoline on Stefan's passion. Within a moment he'd stripped off his own clothes and carried her to one of the couches and followed her down. She exulted in the weight of his body, propped on his elbows, against hers. His chest was hard and his kisses were a delicious combination of soft and passionate.

He plucked her nipples with his fingers then followed with his lips. One of his hands skimmed down over her rib cage, over her abdomen, then lower, between her legs. Everything he did made her feel more restless, more eager, more needy.

She arched toward him and he growled in approval. "Just a moment," he promised and put on protection, then pushed her legs apart.

She instinctively braced herself just before he thrust inside her. "Oh," she whispered, at the stinging, stretching sensation.

Stefan abruptly paused and searched her face. "Eve, are you—"

"Not now," she said, feeling self-conscious for the first time since he'd begun kissing her.

"Why didn't you—"

She tugged on his shoulders to draw his face closer to hers. "Can we talk about this later?" she asked and wriggled experimentally beneath him.

Stefan swore. "Stop it," he said, but brushed his lips over her jaw.

"Why? I think I'm starting to like—"

He covered her mouth with his and began to pump slowly inside her, stealing her breath. He slid his fingers between their lower bodies, stroking her at the same time. Eve felt as if she were a rubber band drawn tighter and tighter. She breathed in sharp bursts, wondering how much longer she could stand the sensation of him filling her and caressing her. A rolling surge of pleasure started in the backs of her legs and moving upward to her lower abdomen, her core, and exploded inside her, rippling throughout her entire body. Her eyes were closed, yet she saw flashes of vibrant colors.

Forcing herself to open her eyes, she looked straight into Stefan's gaze and saw the instant he climaxed. His eyes flashed with fire and he jerked, a giant spasm shooting from him into her. On top of her own pleasure, it was almost too much, physically, emotionally. She clung to him for several moments.

She finally caught her breath and whispered, "Wow."

"Yes," he said, his face pressed into her shoulder. "Wow."

He took another breath and rolled to his side, his arms

still wrapped around her. "Why didn't you tell me?" he asked.

"Tell you what?" she asked.

He lifted a dark eyebrow, but said nothing aloud. His expression did all the talking for him.

Eve sighed. "You mean that I'm not sexually experienced," she said. "Did I not satisfy you?"

He swore. "You know that's not an issue," he said. "I'm more concerned about the fact that I took your virginity."

"You didn't take it," she said. "I gave it. And trust me, if I hadn't wanted to give it, I wouldn't have." She glanced up at the swirling fans circling against the ceiling. "I've had opportunities, but it never seemed right. Or the men never seemed right. Or I just didn't want them enough. Sex isn't something I take lightly. I know there are risks. I never met any man worth the risk until you," she said and looked at him.

He met her gaze for a long moment. "Because I'm royal?"

Eve rolled her eyes. "You really are stuck on that, aren't you? You just don't get it, do you? I've never met a man who I felt was as strong as I was." She shook her head. "Oh, forget it," she muttered and started to climb off the couch.

Stefan's arm closed around her like a vise, then he turned her toward him. "Give me a break. I've never been with a woman like you."

"Is that good or bad?" she asked.

He paused a half beat. "I haven't figured it out yet—"

Hurt, she tried to roll away from him, but he stopped her. "Good Lord, you have no sense of humor."

She shot him a fulminating glare. "If I said the same to you?"

"Okay," he said. "You're good and bad for me. Good for my soul, good for my heart. Bad for my self-control. There. Does that help?"

"Does that mean you want me to go away?" she asked, her eyes dark with both questions and passion.

"Don't even think about it," he said and pulled her on top of him.

Eve's heart hammered against her chest. Every naked inch of him was impressed against every naked inch of her. She slid her fingers through his hair and lowered her mouth to his, exulting in every millimeter of the flesh of his lips. She licked them and sucked them, kissed them and started all over.

Stefan groaned. "Eve, I can't stand this," he muttered, pressing against her intimately so she knew what he meant.

"What do you want?" she whispered.

"Inside you," he said without waiting a half beat.

"What are you waiting for?" she asked.

Letting out a long groan, he put on another condom and pulled her down on his aching shaft. She moaned. He groaned again.

He guided her hips over him and Eve found herself loving this ride more than any other she'd experienced. After a few moments, however, she felt herself tighten in anticipation. A combination of neediness and want consumed her. "Stefan," she said, sensations intensifying with each passing moment. She sank down on him at the same time he thrust inside her and she felt a spasm of pleasure radiate from her core to every other place inside her. One heartbeat later, he thrust inside her again

with a loud groan of satisfaction that vibrated throughout her.

"Oh. Wow," she managed in a broken whisper.

"Oh. Yes," he said, wrapping his arms around her as
if he never intended to let her go. And a secret part of
her hoped it was true.

She secretly wished he wanted her at least half as
much as she wanted him.... And that wish could be
dangerous.

Stefan awakened with Eve wrapped around him. He
glanced around the room for a clock and finally spotted
one. 2:00 a.m. For goodness' sake, why had he fallen
asleep? And for this long?

The sensation of her silky leg twined with his kept
him pinned to the couch. Her hair splayed across her
face in waves, her eyelashes looked like a mysterious
dark fan against her cheeks. Remembering how good it
had felt to take her, to be inside her, aroused him again.
Since he needed to jet out for an early-morning meeting
in France, he couldn't give in to the urge.

"Eve," he said in a low voice. "Wake up, sweetheart."

She wiggled against him and sighed, still dead to the
world.

Her breasts brushing his chest made him clench his
jaw. It would be so easy to kiss her awake, caress her
and sink inside... He cut off the thought.

"Eve," he repeated, in a normal voice. "We
need—"

Her eyes blinked open and she stared at him. She let
out a scream and punched his face and kicked at him.
"Get away from me! Get away—"

Shocked, and his cheekbone stinging, Stefan quickly

backed away from her flailing arms and feet. "What the bloody hell? What's wrong with you?"

Sitting straight up, she blinked and shook her head. "Stefan?"

"Of course, it's me. Who did you think it was?" he demanded.

"I didn't know. I was having this dream and suddenly I woke up and a man was on top of me. It terrified me." She glanced down at herself, taking quick shallow breaths, still clearly disoriented. "Oh, my God, I'm completely naked." She grabbed a pillow and held it against her as she closed her eyes and tried to calm herself.

"Are you okay?" he asked, moving toward her warily. Bloody hell, the woman had a hard right punch.

"This is embarrassing," she said. "I just hit you, didn't I?"

"Yes."

"I'm so sorry. I'm just not used to waking up to find a man beside me," she said.

He gingerly rubbed his cheek again. "No need to prove that to me."

She cringed, rising to her feet, lifting her hand to his cheek. "Is it okay?"

"Of course it is," he said, capturing her hand and brushing aside the pain. "But we do need to leave. I'm making a three-day trip to France and I have meetings first thing in the morning."

"Oh, what time is it?" she asked, glancing around the room.

"Just after two," he said.

She looked at him in horror. "How could we have both fallen asleep like that?"

He chuckled. "One of the secrets to a good night's sleep is great sex, and I'd say that's what we had in spades."

A twinge of self-consciousness flashed across her eyes before she glanced away. "I should get dressed. What a night," she muttered, nearly tripping over an ottoman.

He caught her against him. "Wait just a moment and let me turn on a light. There's no need to be embarrassed."

"I'm not," she retorted quickly.

Releasing her, he turned on a lamp and began to dress himself.

"Okay, maybe a little. I haven't done this before," she said and scooped up her clothing. "I feel—flustered." She made a sound of frustration. "I'm never flustered."

He walked to her and put his hand under her chin, forcing her to meet his gaze. The turbulent emotion he saw in her eyes pulled hard at his gut. She was strong, but she was vulnerable. For a moment, he wondered if he should have allowed himself to take her. She wasn't as sophisticated as his other lovers had been. He also knew, however, that what had been building between them wouldn't have gone away.

"Don't be so hard on yourself. This was your first time," he said.

She growled and lifted her chin away from his hand. "Oh, good grief. It's not like I was a sixteen-year-old virgin." She stepped into her panties and pulled her dress over her head, then balled her bra into a knot. "Where's my purse?" she muttered, looking around the room.

Spotting it close to the glass doors, he collected it and gave it to her. "Here."

"Thanks," she said, snatching it from him and cramming her bra into her purse.

"I'll be back from Paris in four days. I'd like to see you," he said.

She looked up at him, shaking her bangs from her eyes. "For what?" she asked and shifted on her feet. "I mean, is this just going to be a sex thing? Am I a mistress or—"

"No," he said. "If you were my mistress, I would set you up in a private apartment and give you a monthly income. Your only purpose in life would be to be available at my beck and call."

She lifted her eyebrows and rounded her lips in an O. "Sounds like you've done this before."

"No. As a matter of fact, I haven't, but my father did several times."

She gave a slow nod.

"You and me and just you and me. As you requested," he said, wondering why his heart was hammering. He wondered if she would suddenly have buyer's remorse and back away from him. He didn't want that. Stefan couldn't remember having a relationship with a more authentic woman in his life.

"But secret," she said.

"Of course. If the press or advisers found out, it would be hell for both of us," he said.

She thought about that for a moment. "So what do you have planned for us in four nights?" she asked, her lips lifting in a slight smile.

"We could go for a ride after dark," he said.

"I'd like that," she said and took a deep breath. "I'm ready to go."

"Good," he said. He slid his hand behind her back to escort her from the room. Part of him, a big part of him, wanted to keep her with him, but he knew he couldn't.

The following day, Bridget stomped into the barn office with two cartons of Chinese food and a laptop. "I'm furious," she said. "He has no right. No right at all. Is cashew shrimp okay with you?" she said more than asked as she plopped the cartons onto Eve's desk. "Do you like Chinese?" she asked with a scowl.

Not my fave, Eve thought, but Bridget was so unhappy she decided to make do. She hadn't planned to eat any lunch at all today.

"Hey, how are you today?" Eve asked.

Bridget opened the carton of food, then lifted a hand. "I know I got a little out of hand last night. Drank a little too much—" She broke off and used chopsticks to take a bite. "But that was no excuse for Stefan using strong-arm tactics and being a party pooper."

"Hmm," Eve said, because she suspected anything else would just get Bridget more fired up.

"It's ridiculous, and I was totally embarrassed that he arranged for another ride home for you because he thought I wouldn't calm down," Bridget added and took another bite. "You and I had a very nice dinner and you weren't miserable at the club." She paused. "Were you?"

Eve squirmed in her seat. "I wasn't really miserable," she began.

Bridget's face fell. "Yes, you were. I'm sorry. I'm just so fed up with all the social appearances I have to make. I needed one night of freedom." She sighed. "I guess I went overboard."

"I'm not familiar with the security requirements...."

Bridget scowled. "They're supposed to know everywhere I go days in advance. That allows for zero spontaneity."

"Hmm," Eve said. "Do you know if there have been any threats—"

"There are always threats," Bridget said. "Lately, our citizens are very frustrated by the lack of jobs."

"That's a problem in lots of places," Eve said.

"Exactly," Bridget said. "But in general the people of Chantaine are very loving and peaceful. I have a hard time believing any of them would commit a violent act against the royal family."

Eve nodded. "But still, the palace security must protect you...."

Bridget sighed. "True. All too true. Maybe I just need a vacation."

Eve thought about what Stefan had said about letting Bridget go to Italy, but she knew she should hold her tongue. "Maybe a break is right around the corner," she said vaguely and took a bite of shrimp from the box.

"I can't bank on that. I'm the number-one girl now, and I don't like it," she confessed. "I don't want to be irresponsible, but I don't know how Valentina managed this. I think Stefan needs a wife."

Strangling over the bite she'd just taken, Eve snapped her head up. "A wife?" she echoed weakly.

"Yes, it's perfect. Stefan needs a wife who can take over the bulk of the royal duties. Then I could just be free. So, I'm starting my research today," she said, booting up her laptop. "If I put enough women in Stefan's path, surely he will want to marry one of them." She clicked on the notebook mouse and swayed the screen toward Eve.

A beautiful, sophisticated blonde appeared on the screen. "A duchess in Sweden. I think Stefan is partial to blondes. He had a passionate affair with a Swedish model a few years ago. What do you think?"

Eve took a sip of water and felt her appetite disappear like a vapor. "I have no idea," she managed and took another sip.

Bridget frowned. "But what do you think of the idea? I think it's a win-win for everyone. He's been so busy during the last two years he hasn't taken the time to have a relationship, and I have to believe a regular love life would improve his disposition."

Eve strangled over the water and set her cup on her desk. "Oh."

"Plus the advisers would be thrilled. The whole country would be thrilled. And when Stefan's new wife takes over the high-profile duties," Bridget said with a cagey smile, "I will be thrilled. So help me select a few contenders. I could invite them here for some beach time and a palace party."

"You're going to invite them all at the same time?" Eve couldn't resist asking. "Maybe you should make it a reality show."

Bridget's eyes glowed with enthusiasm. "What a fabulous idea."

"I was joking," Eve said. "I'm not sure Stefan would appreciate your manipulating his love life. How would you feel if he did the same to you?"

Bridget waved her hand. "Oh, he's done it to me a thousand times. I'm surprised he didn't try to get me engaged before I hit puberty. Stefan wants all of us to marry in a way that benefits Chantaine. When he finally gets around to getting married, I'm sure he'll choose a woman who can benefit the country in a multitude of ways."

"I realize it's not my place to ask, but what about love?" Eve asked.

Bridget shrugged. "I'm not sure love comes into it. Whoever he marries will bear a ton of duty and responsibility. High-profile appearances, bearing children, never publicly disagreeing with Stefan."

"That lets me out," Eve muttered.

"Pardon?" Bridget said.

"That lets any woman like me out of the running. If I strongly disagree, I can't hide it," she said.

Bridget giggled. "Now, that's the funniest thing I've heard in days. You and Stefan together? The advisers would fall over in one swoop. I wouldn't be surprised if an earthquake wouldn't swallow the palace whole."

"Glad I could amuse you," Eve said drily, then shook her head. "I'm glad I'm not Stefan. I would like to marry for love."

Bridget turned sober. "Hmm. The crown princes have always married for duty and often had mistresses on the side. My father did, as did his father."

"Didn't that bother your mother?" Eve asked.

"I think she was totally enamored with my father in the beginning. We don't discuss this, but she was second choice. His first love bailed on him. My mother definitely did her part in the child-bearing department. Not so much the child-rearing. My father was a playboy from the time he was a teenager until the last couple of years of his life."

"And Stefan is determined to live down that reputation," Eve mused.

Bridget nodded. "Exactly. All the more reason I should help him." She clicked her mouse and a photo of another gorgeous woman flashed up on the screen. "What do you think of her?"

"I can't help you, Bridget. I've got horses to train," she said and stood.

"But you haven't eaten the lunch I brought you," Bridget protested. "Come on, this could be enormous fun. Much more fun than working on a charity fundraiser."

"I'll help you with a charity fundraiser, but I'm not touching this."

"I'll hold you to it," she said and shoved her laptop into her pink bag. She grabbed her carton of Chinese. "We'll talk later. Ta-ta for now. If you won't help me select Stefan's future bride, then I'll just get a facial."

For the next few days, Eve brooded over everything Bridget had told her about Stefan. She wondered about his past affairs. She wondered what he wanted in a wife. She wondered why in the world he was involved with her. She was not blonde, not pedigreed, not submissive or politically correct.

It wasn't as if this was a long-term relationship, she reminded herself, even though the thought pinched. It was just something they had to do. For some inexplicable reason, they had to be with each other for this time. However short it was.

Stefan managed to leave Paris a couple hours earlier than planned. After an intense week of meetings with various diplomats and businessmen, he was looking forward to a relaxing evening with Eve. One of his long-time advisers, Tomas, however was determined to receive a detailed account of his trip. Stefan sent a text to Eve to save room for a late dinner during their ride on the beach.

"We must provide more jobs for our people. We must improve our economy," Tomas said.

"I'm working on that nonstop," Stefan said. "But you know I haven't had the cooperation I've needed."

"True," Tomas conceded, nodding his white head in response. "You're much more of a fighter than your father was. The people are afraid to believe but want to hope."

"I won't be taking a trip on the royal yacht with a bunch of playboy bunnies anytime soon," Stefan said.

Tomas nodded. "Speaking of women, though, the time has come for you to find a wife. It would benefit everyone, including you."

"That's way down the list for me, Tomas," Stefan said.

"It shouldn't be," Tomas insisted, drawing his scraggly eyebrows into a frown. "The other advisers and I have some suggestions for you to consider."

Stefan shook his head. "That's not necessary."

"Oh, but it is," Tomas said. "I'd like you to escort one of our candidates at the royal dinner next week."

Stefan sighed. "You know I'll have no time to entertain a woman, let alone talk to her."

"You have no need for concern," Tomas said. "The other advisers and I will help."

Great, Stefan thought. The candidate would be entertained by a bunch of geezers. Any woman in her right mind would run screaming. "Fine, fine," he said, glancing at his watch. "We'll discuss more at our next meeting." He stood. "Thank you very much for coming, Tomas. As always, your loyalty humbles me."

Tomas also stood. "I am proud to serve you, sir."

As soon as Tomas left, Stefan raced to his quarters, giving instructions to the kitchen as he changed clothes. As he walked out of his room, a staff member delivered a basket with food.

"Thank you," Stefan said.

"Your Highness," the staff member said. "Are you sure you wouldn't prefer another staff member to carry the basket for you?"

Stefan chuckled. "I think I can manage. Have a good evening."

"Yes, sir. You, too," the kitchen boy said.

Stefan smiled. "I'll do my best." He'd already informed security of his plans for the evening. A car pulled up next to the private exit as he stepped outside the door. Despite his long day of travel, he could have easily jogged to the stables, but riding in the car would appease security. Less than five minutes later, he arrived at the stables.

"Sir, are you sure you don't want us to bring the basket for you?" Franco asked.

"I know I seem feeble, but I can manage it," Stefan cracked.

Franco unsuccessfully muffled a chuckle. "Sir, you are anything but feeble. I ask only for your convenience."

"To be perfectly honest, Franco, I don't want you anywhere near me tonight," Stefan said. "In fact, I'm going to pretend you don't exist."

"Point taken, sir," Franco responded. "We will be invisible."

"Thank you," he said and stepped out of the car. He walked inside the stable and heard the sound of Eve's voice. He paused, listening to her coo at Gus. He heard Black stomping in his stall, almost as if he were jealous. Heaven help him, he understood. He, too, wanted

Eve cooing over him. Ridiculous, he thought and strode toward her.

She must have heard him because she turned and her eyes lit, making him feel alive inside. "Welcome back," she said. "How was France? Eat any croissants for me?"

He stepped toward her, dropped the basket and pulled her into his arms. "It's good to see you. Only one croissant. I spent half my time wondering what you would think of Paris."

"And the other half?" she asked.

"Working," he said. "Tell me you missed me."

"A little," she said.

He kissed her, and she sighed.

"Okay, a lot. How'd you score the basket of food so quickly?" she asked.

He shrugged. "I have a few connections." He glanced at Gus, already saddled and ready to go. "How's Black?"

"Ready for a ride," she said with a meaningful nod. "I didn't saddle him because I didn't want to try his patience."

"It won't take me a moment," he said.

Chapter Seven

Stefan watched Eve ride the horse with a combination of grace and sensuality that mesmerized him. He couldn't help remembering the way she'd ridden him, bringing both of them to incredible, forbidden pleasure. He wanted her again. Worse, he craved her. She'd made him feel whole and fulfilled. The sensation couldn't last, he assured himself, for Eve or him. But until it faltered, he was determined to keep her.

He allowed her to lead the way on the path to the beach even though Black protested. He clearly wanted the alpha role. Stefan would allow that on the return ride.

As soon as they hit sand, however, Gus began to run. Seconds later, Black followed, easily passing Gus. A few seconds later, Stefan saw the fire his staff had built in preparation for his evening with Eve. He reined in Black.

Hearing the slowing hoofbeats of Gus, he glanced over his shoulder and saw Eve reining in her mount. She glanced at the fire. "How did this happen?" she asked.

"I'm a magician," he said. "I wish for it and," he snapped his fingers, "it happens."

She paused a second. "You're full of bull."

He laughed. "Just sharing a legend. Myths and legends are important."

"Maybe," she said skeptically, but dismounted. "Is this when we eat?"

"Sounds like a good time to me," he said and dismounted Black. As soon as Eve slid off of her mount, he led both horses to a tree and tied them to it. "Behave," he said to Black and patted the horse.

Turning around, he looked at her as she sat on the blanket. She'd removed her black Stetson and her hair splayed over her shoulders and down her back. With the fire lighting her skin, she glanced up at him and her lips tilted in a mysterious smile, making him wonder what she was thinking.

She looked into the basket and pulled out the sandwiches the chef had prepared, along with the bottle of wine and chocolates. "Not bad, but I imagine this is a step down from Paris."

"Not at all," he said, sinking to the blanket beside her. "The company is far superior."

Her smile grew. "Oops. You're being charming. I better watch out." She unwrapped a sandwich while he poured the wine into two glasses. "Was the trip successful?"

He nodded. "Three of the consultants are committed to working on events that will include Chantaine." He gave her a glass of wine and clicked his against hers.

"Enough about my trip. What has been happening here since I left?"

"The veterinary specialist came to evaluate Black as a stud," she said.

"And?" he asked.

"In human language, he's quite virile and has the capacity to make many prize foals."

He grinned at her evaluation. "There's more value in being one of many."

"One?" she said, in exasperation. "You're not suggesting that Black should only sire one foal?"

"No, but we will be very selective about which mares will be allowed to carry on his line."

She relaxed slightly. "No problem. I'm sure we can get the best mares lining up for a stud anytime you say the word." She swirled the wine in her glass. "Speaking of stud service, your sister has decided you need a wife. She's putting together a list of prospects to…relax you."

The notion of Bridget having a clue about what kind of woman he would want was so hilarious that he roared with laughter. He quickly noticed that Eve didn't share his amusement.

"You realize how ridiculous that is, don't you?" he asked her.

"You need to get married sometime," Eve said with a shrug. "You need a wife to perform all the royal duties including continuing your family's line."

"Now you're sounding like the advisers," he muttered and took another sip of wine.

"They want you to get married, too?" she asked.

"They've wanted me to get married since I turned twenty-one. You have no idea how many times I've heard the line 'for the good of the country' when it comes to my love life," he said.

Surprise flickered across her face. "You seem to embrace all of your other duties easily enough. Why shirk this one?"

"I'm not shirking it. I just refuse to be pushed into it. I have plenty of time," he said. "If you see my name matched with a woman, rest assured it's wishful thinking."

"So there's no fiancée waiting in the wings," she said. "Because I wouldn't want to feel like I'm—poaching."

He leaned toward her and slid his hand behind her neck to bring her lips closer to his. "You're not," he said and lowered his mouth to hers.

They enjoyed a companionable meal and a walk along the edge of the ocean. He slid his hand through hers, liking the combination of calluses and smooth skin. "Are you still homesick for Texas?"

"Some," she confessed. "I miss my aunt and the familiarity of everything there. And barbecue. There's no barbecue here."

"I'm sure the chef could prepare barbecue—"

"Don't you be giving your chef any extra work because of me. He has enough to do pleasing you, your sisters and guests," she fussed.

"Our chef is accustomed to preparing dishes for all our international guests. Why should you be any different?" he asked.

"I'm not a guest," she said. "I'm staff."

He scoffed. "Maybe *I* want barbecue," he said.

She laughed and the sound created a ripple of pleasure inside him. "You're crazy."

"Maybe," he said and pulled her against him, inhaling her scent. "It's good to see you, to be with you tonight."

Her gaze met his and she nodded. "It is." She closed her eyes for a second, then opened them. "It's almost magical, the breeze, the time alone...."

His gut twisted and he was filled with a shocking longing to steal Eve away for a week or more away from everyone and everything. His schedule was packed. It was impossible. But it didn't keep him from wanting. He allowed himself another taste of her, taking her lips and kissing her.

She slipped her arms around him and he felt the thud of arousal in his blood. If he were anyone else, he would take her on the beach with the breeze kissing their skin and the sound of the surf flowing over them. But he wasn't someone else. He was the Crown Prince of Chantaine, and he refused to be the same kind of man his father had been. Hearing Black snort and paw, Stefan held Eve against him for a long moment, then released her reluctantly. "We should go. The horses are getting restless," he said.

They returned to the barn and each put away their mounts. Stefan ached with the need to bring Eve back to his suite with him, but he wanted her one way: willing. He kissed her lightly on the lips, then moved away. Any longer would have presented too much of a temptation. "I don't want you to feel like I'm giving you a booty call, so the next move is yours. You have my cell number. You can call or text me."

Eve gaped at him. "Excuse me?"

"I said, you make the next move. Thank you for a wonderful evening. I've instructed one of my security to escort you to your quarters. Good night," he said and turned away.

"We don't do that in Texas," she said, stopping him mid-stride.

He turned around. "You don't do what?" he asked.

She *almost* squirmed. "Women don't give booty calls."

Amused, he lifted an eyebrow. "You're not in Texas anymore."

She shook her head and gave a sound of frustration. "How exactly am I supposed to give a crown prince a booty call?"

Pleased that she was interested in calling him, he smiled. "You'll figure it out. Ciao, Beautiful."

"I'm not beautiful," she called after him.

"Come to my bed and you'll never say that again," he said over his shoulder and let her stew over that. He knew she would. It was small comfort considering he would be taking an ice-cold shower before he went to bed tonight.

Exasperated beyond sanity, Eve stared after him as he walked away and stuck out her tongue. *As if* she would ever give a booty call to anyone, let alone a prince. It didn't matter who it was, she just wouldn't do it. She stomped around the barn, doing a last check on the horses, then turned out all the lights except one. Still grumpy, she stared at the door where she'd last seen his smart, sensual mouth curve into a sexy smile and stuck out her tongue again.

Someone cleared their throat, scaring the wits out of her. "Who is it? Who's there?"

"It's Max Roberts, ma'am, with his Royal Highness's security," an extremely fit gray-haired man said as he stepped from the shadows. "I'm sorry if I startled you. His Highness requested that I escort you to your quarters."

"How long have you been here?" she asked suspiciously.

"Since His Royal Highness departed the building," he said.

"Oh, great," she said. "I suppose you'll tell him all about the fact that I stuck out my tongue at him."

Max's lips barely twitched. "It would bring me great joy, but I wouldn't dream of bringing you any pain."

She laughed, despite her discomfort. "A gentleman," she said. "How did I get so lucky?"

"A beautiful American," he echoed. "How did I get so lucky?" He paused a half beat. "Don't worry. I'm not hitting on you. You're just loads more interesting than most of the visitors I'm asked to escort."

"Such as?" she asked, moving toward him.

"I'm not at liberty to disclose that information."

"Discreet," she said. "You're a man after my own heart. Take me home, Max. Any insider info you can give me on His Highlyness?"

"You just said you appreciated discretion," he said as he led her out the door.

"Yes, but there's a difference between discretion and stinginess," she said, because she had to try.

"What kind of music do you like, Ms. Jackson?" he asked, clearly changing the station.

"Stingy it is," she said with a sigh.

That night, Eve tossed and turned. She threw the covers off of her, then dragged them back over her. Her dreams held images of Stefan. She ran to him, but then he disappeared. By the time she awakened before dawn, she was completely cranky. Sipping a cup of coffee after her shower, she scowled at her cell phone. Why did she have to be the one to call? She scowled again.

Through her irritable mind, an idea occurred to her. The more she thought about it, the more she liked it. Taking a deep breath, she gathered her wits and dialed Stefan's number.

"Good morning, Ms. Jackson," he said, sounding far more awake than she did. "How are you?"

"Great," she said, her heart racing. "And you?"

"I'm good. What can I do for you?"

"May I join you for breakfast?"

A silence passed, and she wondered if she had made a mistake. "Or not," she said. "If it's not convenient and—"

"I would like that very much. How soon can you join me?" he asked.

She raked her hand through her damp hair and glanced at her robe. "Twenty minutes?"

"Make it ten," he said. "And take the north entrance using the pass code of 3663. See ya," he said, mocking her Texas drawl before he disconnected the call.

Eve stared at her cell phone, then shook her head. "Nine minutes," she muttered and stripped off her towel as she headed for her bedroom. She dressed in clothes for work with her hair drying in damp waves. Clamping her hat on her head, she dashed out her apartment door and ran down the stairs to the narrow cobblestone road. She rushed, then realized she shouldn't, and deliberately slowed her gait. Entering the code, she pushed the door open and climbed the stairs to Stefan's suite.

She barely knocked on the door before he opened the door, dressed in an unbuttoned white shirt and black slacks. She suspected a tie and meetings were in his future.

"I'm impressed. You almost made it on time," he said and motioned her inside.

She removed her hat and shook her head. "It occurred to me that a gentleman should never rush a woman, and ten minutes is rushing."

"The rush was for me," he said. "I wanted as much time with you as possible. Full American breakfast."

Eve saw the table set with fine china and sterling-covered serving dishes and was stunned. "Do you do this every day?"

"Absolutely not," he said. "I have boiled eggs, a protein shake or a protein bar." He lifted one of the sterling covers. "And never ever sausage gravy and biscuits."

Eve was flattered beyond words. "Sausage gravy and biscuits?" she echoed. "I don't know what to say."

"Don't," he said. "Just eat and remember a protein bar is in your future tomorrow."

She laughed and looked down at the table. "Yes, Your Highlyness."

"That name is irritating to me," he said.

"My aunt coined it with your sister Valentina," she said and dug in to her meal. "It's a term of affection."

"Why don't I believe you?" he asked.

"Because you're a suspicious, jaded, cynical man?" she asked and took a bite of a biscuit with gravy that was almost as good as her aunt's. "This is so good. Almost as good as—"

"Your aunt Hildie's?" he asked, taking a bite of eggs and biscuit. "She gave the recipe to the chef when she visited with Valentina."

Eve laughed. "So like her. She left something out. I can taste it."

Stefan frowned. "What? She tricked my chef?"

"Not exactly tricked," Eve said. "She just didn't tell all. Think about it. You don't always tell all, do you?"

"Such as?" he asked.

"Just curious," she said. "How serious was that relationship you had with the Swedish model a few years ago?"

Stefan groaned. "Maja. Big mistake. Drama queen, and after we'd become involved, she decided she wanted to be Crown Princess of Chantaine."

"You broke her heart," she said.

"Hardly," he said. "Two days after we broke it off, she was in the papers with a French billionaire. Soon after, she got pregnant with his daughter and they got married."

"Were you heartbroken?" she asked.

"I came to my senses," he said.

The same way he would come to his senses about me, she thought and deliberately pushed it aside. "Just curious. What was so wrong about her?"

"You're very curious this morning. Are you this way every morning?" he asked.

She smiled. "I rarely have such amazing company for breakfast. You didn't answer my question."

He folded his hands together and met her gaze. "For a true marriage, I believe a man and woman must connect on several levels, physically, emotionally, intellectually. Maja and I didn't have that. My father was dying at the time. She provided a temporary diversion, but it wasn't enough to go the distance. I knew it at the start and told her exactly how I felt."

Eve smiled slowly. "In that way, you're like a Texan. We're not big on pretending."

He nodded. "What do you have planned today?" he asked, changing the subject.

"The farrier is coming. I'm working on some gait issues with one of the geldings. I'll put Black through his paces if you don't plan to ride tonight."

"That would be a good idea. What do you have planned for the evening?" he asked.

"What part of the evening?" she asked. "Dinner? Bedtime?"

"Evening," he repeated, his gaze causing all kinds of jittery sensations inside her.

She set down her fork and folded her hands in her lap. "Well, I'm a Texas lady," she said. "And we don't believe in chasing men. We don't make booty calls. I made a breakfast call," she said. "The ball is in your court."

Stefan smiled. "Rascal woman."

She met his gaze. "Who, me?"

"Okay, you've forced my hand. Meet me in my quarters at 10:00 p.m."

"That's pretty late for this working girl," she said.

"I have a working dinner with a visitor from Egypt. Would you like to join us?"

"Ten, it is," she said and put her hat on her head and stood. "Please give my compliments to your chef. Marvelous breakfast."

"I'll pass along your compliments. Maybe you can shake loose a few secrets from your aunt about her favorite recipes," he said, standing.

"Good luck with that," Eve said. "She can be a little ornery at times."

"Just like her niece," he said.

"If you're going to compare me to my aunt Hildie, you've given me a huge compliment," Eve said.

He nodded and walked toward her, tilting her hat off her head. "Interesting version of a booty call."

"It wasn't a booty call," she protested. "It was a breakfast call."

"Close enough," he said and then pressed his mouth against hers. "Best morning I've had in a long time. You can work on the booty part later."

Eve kept herself busy until dusk, which in this case was 8:00 p.m. She'd eaten a peanut butter and jelly sandwich with lots of water. She took a shower and would have normally gotten into bed and read before she fell asleep. Tonight, she dressed in a sundress but still thought about her pj's. She thought more intensely as each moment passed. Her cell rang at nine-thirty. Stefan.

"Would you join me for a cocktail on my balcony?" he asked.

She took a deep breath. That sounded so much better than a booty call.

"A Texas Rose?" he asked, and her mind turned to the romantic night they'd shared.

"I'm good with water tonight," she said.

He gave a low chuckle that rolled over her nerve endings like honey. "I have plenty of that. Max will arrive to escort you in a few moments."

"That's not necessary," she said.

"Yes, it is," he said firmly.

Just as Stefan had said, Max arrived a few minutes later and walked her to the palace door. "Enjoy your evening, Ms. Jackson."

"If I call you Max, then you can call me Eve. Thanks for the escort," she said and made her way up the stairs to Stefan's quarters. Her heart hammering in her chest, she lightly knocked on the door.

He opened it immediately and ushered her inside.

"Good evening, beautiful," he said and pulled her into his arms. "Is the dress for me?"

She felt herself flush with self-consciousness followed quickly by a prickle of irritation. "No. I was actually planning on clubbing tonight. You called right before I planned to leave," she said, tongue in cheek.

"Clubbing," he said with a frown then studied her face and laughed. "You're a bloody tease, Eve Jackson."

"Not at all," she said. "You're just too accustomed to everyone tripping over themselves to try to please you."

"Funny you don't have to try, yet you still do," he said thoughtfully, then pulled back and waved toward the balcony. "Come out. I have a little surprise for you."

Curious, she followed him outside and saw a table set with bottled water, milk and a plate of cookies. She felt a twist of nostalgia. "Oh, my aunt used to fix this as a snack for me whenever I visited her. Are they chocolate chip?" she asked, sinking into the chair he offered.

He nodded and took the chair next to her. "Since you weren't interested in a Texas Rose, I thought you might like a different taste of home."

"How did you know?" she asked and took a bite of the cookie.

"I have ways," he said.

She studied him suspiciously. "You talked to Hildie again, didn't you?"

"You know how tight my schedule has been. When have I had time to call your aunt?" he asked.

"True," she said. "But you could have gotten someone else to call her. Thank you," she said.

"I never said I did it," he said.

"Okay," she conceded, but was secretly thrilled that he would have gone to such trouble to please her.

"What was your favorite bedtime snack when you were a kid?"

"My diet was zealously monitored by a strict nanny from the time I was eight until I went away to school at age twelve."

Eve winced. "That doesn't sound like much fun."

His lips twitched. "I had sources. It wasn't a bedtime snack, but I wanted peanut M&M's and Skittles as often as I could get them. One of my uncles slipped me some on occasion. I hoarded them."

Eve laughed at the image. "Oh, my gosh, and I would have thought you'd been given everything you wanted."

He met her gaze for a heartbeat that made her lose her breath. "You would have been wrong." Glancing away, he took a drink of his water. "I can't deny I was given a life of enormous privilege, but for some reason, my family always felt fractured. We didn't feel like a family. Valentina and I were closer than the rest. I keep trying to make us more of a family, but sometimes I wonder if it's too late."

Her heart twisted and she realized what her gut had told her. She and Stefan shared more than anyone would believe possible at first, or even second, glance. She knew the pain of a family that just couldn't seem to come together. She lifted her hand and covered his. "Some people would say it's never too late."

"What about you?" he asked.

"I work at believing, but it's tough. My mother and father were a dysfunctional mess."

"Mine were, too," he said.

"But they had six children together," she said.

"The duty of progeny," he said.

"Six?" she said in disbelief. "There's duty and there's duty."

He leaned back and sighed. "My father wanted to marry someone else, but the woman dumped him. My mother was supposedly second choice. I think the first five years they gave it their best. After that, my mother tried to keep his interest by having more children. Jacques was her last desperate attempt. My father took mistresses on a regular basis and their marriage became more of a business arrangement."

"Did she love him?"

"She was a very young and innocent French countess when they married, twelve years younger than him. Nineteen years old on the day they married. I'm sure she was enamored by his position, excited to be the object of adulation from the people of Chantaine and at times, the rest of the world."

"Nineteen. Wow, that was young."

He nodded.

"How do you feel about the whole taking-a-mistress thing?" she asked.

"Why do you think I'm delaying marriage?" he returned. "I don't want the same kind of relationship when I take a wife. It may be damn hard, but I want a real family."

"I understand that. You think the odds are against you?" she asked. "I figure with my background, they're against me."

"Possibly," he said. "I've heard that expression you Americans use. The apple doesn't fall far from the tree. But I'm already a different man than my father was. A different leader with different goals. I'll do what it takes to be taken seriously so I can improve my country. I won't be marrying a *Playboy* model or beauty-contest winner. I won't choose a wife purely on the basis of her title or her beauty."

"Good for you," she said. "You and I have that in common. I won't be marrying a *Playgirl* model or a boy toy. Well," she added in a light, mocking tone, "unless he worships the ground I walk on and knows how to fix amazing baby back ribs."

"Baby back ribs?" he echoed. "I think I remember Valentina talking about ribs when she attended college in Texas."

"If she was referring to baby back ribs, she wasn't talking," Eve said. "She was moaning, saying oooohhh, ahhhh...I want more."

Stefan narrowed his eyes. "What the hell is the recipe for these ribs? Do they have some kind of aphrodisiac in their flavoring?"

She laughed. "No. They're just amazingly delicious and there are a gajillion recipes. People get into fistfights over what's the best way to fix ribs."

"Sounds primitive," he said.

"And redneck," she added. "But once you've tried to fix them, you become a redneck."

"This sounds like one of the exclusive fraternities at university that I refused to join," he said.

She shrugged. "Bet they didn't know a thing about fixing ribs."

He gave a slow smile and folded his hand around hers. "True. Learning how to cook ribs was not a priority for the students at Oxford."

"Well, that shows you how education is deteriorating even in the U.K.," she said, making a *tsk*-ing sound and shaking her head.

Stefan gave her a sharp tug and pulled her onto his

lap. "Thank God you're here to correct my deficient education," he said.

His low chuckle against her ear sent a ripple of pleasure through her body. "I live to serve," she managed, a little more breathlessly than she intended.

"Yeah, right," he said, chuckling again. Then he cupped her chin and looked deep into her eyes. "Stay with me for a while."

Eve felt herself sinking into him. She could have fought it. Well, she liked to believe that she could have fought it. But when she looked into his eyes, the word *no* was completely absent from her vocabulary.

Chapter Eight

"You're coming to dinner tonight at the palace," Bridget said in a singsong voice with a wide smile as she made her way into Eve's office at the stable the next day mid-morning. It never ceased to amaze Eve how Bridget seemed to ignore the fact that her high heels weren't a good match for the dirt floor of the stable. Bridget was currently wearing a hot-pink shirtdress, a pink hat and pink shoes. Bless her heart, the princess looked like a cartoon.

"Just curious, where have you been? Where are you going?" Eve asked.

"A visit at a home for the elderly. Yes, I know I look ridiculous, but it's cheery," she said. "Now, about dinner," she said.

Eve shook her head. "Bridget, I really appreciate the invite, but—"

"No buts," she said. "I'll be bored out of my mind

without you. Do you realize no one else within ten years of my age will be attending? Have a little pity, Eve."

"What about Phillipa?"

"The sneak got out of it, said she was working on her dissertation. Convenient excuse."

Eve groaned. "I don't have anything to wear," she said.

Bridget shrugged and smiled. "That's what shopping is for."

"I have work to do," Eve said firmly.

"As do I," Bridget said, lifting her chin. "You have the cute little black dress, but we should get you another option. Give me your measurements and I'll call one of my assistants."

Eve just stared at the woman.

Bridget wrinkled her brow. "Come along. Don't be shy. I don't have all day. Your measurements?" Bridget sighed. "Okay, just send them to my assistant, Helga. This is her number," she said, scratching the number on a piece of paper on Eve's desk. "Don't worry. She'll take your size to the grave. Our security could learn lessons from this woman. Tonight, 7:00 p.m. at the Serrisa Ballroom."

"I didn't say—"

"Too late. You didn't say no, so that means yes. You won't regret it. I'll make sure you're entertained. If you haven't called Helga with your measurements by two, then I'll make an arbitrary selection for your dress. Ciao, darling," she said and strutted away.

Eve stared after her thinking this Devereaux clan would try the patience of a saint, and heaven knew she was no saint.

* * *

Hours later, Eve dressed in a cream-colored gown and nude sandals. Helga had also sent a tiara, but that was just way over the top for Eve. She stared at herself in the mirror and felt like Cinderella going to the ball. Or like she was dressing up for Halloween. Either was uncomfortable. She picked up her cell to call Bridget. Her phone rang, surprising her so much she nearly dropped her phone.

"Hello," she said before she looked at the return number.

"No reneging," Bridget said firmly.

Eve sighed. "Bridget, this just isn't me."

"Oh, get over yourself. Pretend you're at a costume party. There will be great food, booze and me for company. Think of this as breaking out of your shell. An escort will pick you up in thirty minutes."

"I could easily walk in that time," Eve said.

"I don't want you to sweat. Sit tight," Bridget said and disconnected the call.

Exactly thirty minutes later, a different security agent appeared outside her building with a car. "Ms. Jackson, I'm Edward. I'll be driving you to the palace for the state dinner tonight."

Eve seriously considered asking him to just take her for a ride along the beach, but she reined in her discomfort. "Thank you, Edward. I'm a first-timer. Any tips?"

"Let the royals go first with everything, and you'll be safe," he said.

"Thanks," she muttered, wishing for milk and cookies. Just a few moments later, however, she walked inside the front door of the palace as opposed to the other entrances she used for her meetings with Stefan. Stepping inside the front hall, she was reminded of the first time she'd entered the palace. It was a stunningly beautiful foyer filled with sparkling crystal chandeliers, marble floors and sculptures. Tonight, the foyer was also filled with women dressed in couture gowns and men in dashing tuxedos.

Eve felt that itchy sensation of not belonging, of being a pretender.

"There you are," Bridget said and moved toward her. The princess wore a spectacular gold dress and tiara. She hooked her arm through Eve's. "Thank goodness you're here. You look fabulous," she said, then frowned. "Where's your tiara?"

"I didn't think it went with the dress," Eve said.

"It was perfect with the dress," Bridget argued.

"I'm not a princess and it made me feel like I *was* dressing for Halloween."

Bridget cackled with laughter. "Okay, you're excused. Bet you think mine is ridiculous."

"You look beautiful," Eve said. "And you can do the crown thing because you're a princess."

Eve gawked at the extravagant jewelry many of the women wore. "Do you think it's real?" she whispered to Bridget. "The diamonds that woman is wearing are the size of golf balls."

Bridget glanced at the older woman and nodded. "That's Princess Margarita from Spain, so yes, they're real. Would you like to meet her?"

"That's okay. I'm happy in the background. You go ahead and do your hostess thing," she said.

"In a moment. I want you to see the woman I'm matching with Stefan first. Come here," she said and nodded toward a tall, stunning blonde. "She's a swimsuit model from Luxembourg. What do you think?"

Eve swallowed over a sudden lump in her throat. "She's beautiful. Can she ride?"

Bridget frowned. "Ride?"

Eve shrugged. "Horseback riding is one of Stefan's passions. I would think he would want his wife to share that passion."

Bridget drew her eyebrows together. "I hadn't thought of that," she mused. "Darn, I hope she doesn't get eliminated because she's afraid of horses."

"Is she?" Eve asked, feeling a terrible, wicked relief.

"I don't know. Hmm. Now that I think of it, Stefan always rides alone. He probably wouldn't want his wife along with him anyway."

If Eve corrected Bridget, then Stefan's sister would want details, which Eve couldn't reveal. Ever. Eve clamped her mouth firmly shut.

"I should go, but I've arranged for you to sit next to me. Get a drink. Mingle. Enjoy yourself," she instructed.

Bridget left in a flourish of silk, and Eve eased her way to the side of the room to people watch. As Bridget said, most of the group appeared to be at least ten years older than she was. The foyer looked different filled with party people. She could almost imagine the same kind of party taking place a century or two ago with the people dressed in different clothes. They would have arrived by carriage instead of limo.

"You look like you're in a different world," a male voice said to her. "Is it more interesting there?"

She blinked and glanced to her side to find a thirty-something dark-haired man looking at her with amusement in his dark eyes. "I was just imagining what a party here might have looked like a hundred years ago."

"Jam-packed with mothers pushing their daughters toward the royal family," he said and took a sip of a drink in a squat glass. "These days the crown prince throws most of these parties for visiting dignitaries, investors or charities."

"And are you a frequent guest at these events?" she asked.

"I'm invited because I bring business to Chantaine. And you?"

"Oh, I'm not really supposed to be here," she said, then corrected herself. "I was invited by Princess Bridget, but I'm really just staff."

"You're an American," he said. "What do you do for the palace?"

"Are you with the press?" she asked. She hadn't forgotten what had happened the last time she talked to a stranger.

He laughed again. "Hell, no. But if you're skittish, we don't have to discuss your occupation."

"I'm not skittish," she said. "I'm the royal stable master."

The man lifted his eyebrows. "Impressive. Stefan prizes his horses."

She studied him. "Do you know him well?"

"Some," he said with a shrug. "My name is Nic Lafitte," he announced, extending his hand. "And you are?"

"Eve Jackson," she said cautiously, allowing him to take her hand. "That name is familiar," she mused, trying to place it.

"Nic?" he asked with a playful grin.

She laughed despite herself and shook her head. "No. Lafitte." She blinked. "That's the name of the famous pirate."

"I thought that was Bluebeard," he said.

"No," she said, laughing again. "Lafitte was the famous pirate in New Orleans. Unusual name. Any relation?"

He extended his hands upward in complete innocence. "Do I look like a pirate?"

Eve studied him and it was easy to imagine him with a pirate's hat, eye patch and boots. "Now that you mention it—"

"Eve, where have you been? It's time for dinner," Bridget said, then glanced at Nic and gave him a hard look. "Mr. Lafitte, what a surprise. I hope you're enjoying the event tonight."

"More than I expected, Your Highness, especially after meeting Ms. Jackson. You're looking more beautiful than ever, Princess Bridget," he said.

"Thank you," Bridget said, but clearly didn't mean it. "Please excuse both of us. We're needed in the dining room."

"I'll be happy to escort Ms. Jackson if you have other duties," he offered.

"Not at all necessary," Bridget said firmly, then grabbed Eve's wrist and rushed away.

"What was that about?" Eve asked as they headed down the hall to the ballroom. "Do you and Nic Lafitte have some sort of romantic history?"

"Absolutely not," Bridget said, with a disdain Eve had never seen her exhibit before. "I would never get involved with a Lafitte. No one in the Devereaux family would. I don't have time to go into it right now, but just trust me. There's a lot of bad blood between the two families."

"Then why in the world would you invite him to your party?"

Bridget sighed as they entered the ballroom. "Because he brings business to Chantaine. Plus he supports many of our local causes."

"Wow, real monster," Eve said, still not understanding.

Bridget lowered her voice. "His great-great-uncle killed a Devereaux, and his father seduced the woman who was originally supposed to marry my father."

Eve digested the information. "Okay, I can see how that could keep them off the Devereaux's BFF list. But if you dislike the Lafittes that much, why would you invite them?"

"We're taking the civilized approach," Bridget said. "Oh, look. Agnes and Stefan are talking. He's nodding. Now, smiling." Bridget gave a mini-applause, then frowned. "What is Countess Laticia doing with Senior Adviser Tomas?"

Eve watched, feeling her stomach sink to her knees. Both women were incredibly beautiful.

"He's matchmaking," Bridget said, indignant. "How is Agnes going to get any time with Stefan if Tomas is pushing a countess at him? Well, I'm fixing this," she muttered, and then took off.

Moments later, it appeared that Agnes would be sitting on one side of Stefan and the young countess on the other. Bridget returned with a triumphant expression on her face. "Much better now," she said. "Agnes deserves a fair fight, wouldn't you say? The games begin."

Eve wished she could be more blasé about the fact that Stefan was surrounded by two women who would do just about anything for his attention, but she felt more miserable with each course of the dinner, and it had nothing to do with the food. She was pretty sure Stefan wasn't even aware of her presence. Why should he be, when he was wedged between a model and a countess?

Bridget chatted with the rest of the table and murmured an observation about Agnes and Stefan every now and then. By the time the waiters were serving dessert, Eve thought she would scream. "I think I need a little air," she said to Bridget. "Please excuse me." She rose from the table and headed straight for the balcony doors. Stepping outside, she gulped in several breaths of fresh air. "Thank God," she whispered.

"That bad?" a male voice said from the shadows. Nic Lafitte stepped forward.

She took another breath and stepped closer to the marble rail. "It's not exactly the backyard barbecue I'm used to," she said.

"Texas," he said triumphantly. "The drawl. I knew you were American and from the South, but I couldn't quite place it. I'm right, aren't I?"

"Yes," she said, wishing she could be alone to collect herself before she thanked Bridget and left for the evening.

"Would you like me to get you a cocktail? You look upset," he said.

"I'm not," she lied. "Just out of my element. I think I'll call it a night."

"Shame," he said, then pulled out a card. "I'm in town every now and then. Give me a call."

She put up her hand. "I don't think so," she said.

"Ah, Bridget ratted on my family," he said. "I'm not all that bad. I'm even part Texan. I own a ranch there."

"So you can play cowboy when the mood strikes?" she asked. She'd heard about men like Nic, who flitted into their ranches from international destinations.

"Can't deny the appeal after spending too much time in meetings," he said. "Bet you even miss it a little."

She did, especially tonight. "I'm going to go now."

"I'll walk you inside," he said, walking with her.

"Thank you, but you don't need to do that," she said.

"I don't have anything else to do," he said, then opened the door.

It was only steps from the balcony into the ballroom. Eve stopped short when she saw Stefan standing a few yards directly in front of her.

"What timing. The prince is making his rounds. He always personally thanks everyone for attending," Nic said.

"He can skip me," she said, stepping backward.

At that moment, Stefan looked up and caught sight of her. And Nic Lafitte. His jaw hardened for a second, and Eve was hoping he would just ignore her. She didn't want to talk to him in this setting. It was surreal and disturbing to her.

Stefan clearly had other ideas as he made a quick comment to his aide and stepped toward her. Eve felt her palms grow damp.

"Ms. Jackson, I wasn't aware you were attending," Stefan said, extending his hand.

She accepted it and gave a little dip that she hoped resembled a curtsy. "Your Highness, Princess Bridget invited me."

"I haven't seen you all evening," he said.

"You've been busy taking care of your—guests," she said, forcing a smile.

He lifted an eyebrow, then turned at Nic. "Thank you for your contributions to Chantaine," he said.

"I consider it my honor and responsibility, Your

Highness. After all, my family has a history with Chantaine. A lovely event tonight, made even lovelier by the presence of Ms. Jackson."

Eve looked at Nic like he was a wack job. *Lovely.* She glanced back at Stefan and noticed that he was clenching his jaw. Interesting, she thought.

"I'm glad you enjoyed the evening. I'll be in touch later," he said to Eve and held her gaze for three seconds before he turned away.

Eve felt as if she'd been scorched and couldn't move.

"Are you sure you're just the stable master?" Nic asked.

"Of course I'm the stable master," she said, praying her face wasn't as red with heat as she thought it was. "Do I look like I could be anything else?"

Nic looked at her for a moment. "You look as if you could be a queen."

"Now I know you're full of it," she said. "I'm going to bed. Have a nice night."

"Are you sure I can't join you?"

"Not in a million years," she said.

"Princess Bridget scared you off," he said.

"It's not that," she said.

"Hmm," he said as if he knew too much.

"Find another girl. I'm sure you won't have a problem. Good night," she said and headed toward Bridget.

She found the princess standing next to Agnes, a physical example of feminine perfection. Bridget turned to her and beamed. "Eve, meet Agnes. Agnes, this is Eve. She's Stefan's new stable master, and we all adore her."

Agnes smiled, revealing perfectly white teeth that

matched every other perfect part of her. "Good evening. You like horses?"

"Yes, thank you, Agnes. Nice to meet you. Your Highness," she said to Bridget, "I'm headed home. Thank you for inviting me."

Bridget pouted. "So soon." She bussed Eve with a kiss on the cheek. "I'll see you tomorrow or the next day. Ciao, Eve."

"Ciao," Eve murmured, and then headed for the door. She picked up the hem of her dress and ran down the hall toward the foyer. Opening the front door, she stepped outside and debated pulling off her shoes.

The chauffeur pulled up to the curb. "Ms. Jackson, would you like a ride to your quarters?"

"Thank you," she said. "That would be wonderful."

The chauffeur stepped outside and helped her into the car. "Did you have a good evening?" he asked.

"Hmm," she said in a noncommittal tone. "I can't wait to get back to my room." She climbed into the car and sank her head against the seat, closing her eyes. What a mistake. She should have never gone tonight. There had been so many times when she hadn't felt as if she'd fit in, and this evening was just one more.

It seemed like only seconds passed and the chauffeur pulled to a stop. "I'll escort you to the door, ma'am," he said.

Eve pulled herself together and stepped from the vehicle. "Thank you," she said and went upstairs to her second-story apartment. Walking inside, she kicked off her shoes and sank onto the sofa. Images of Agnes, the countess and Stefan flashed through her mind like a slide show. She groaned, willing her disturbing thoughts aside. "Never again," she told herself, pushing herself to stand. Maybe a shower would wash the night from her head so she could sleep in peace.

A knock sounded on her door and she frowned. Who? At this time of night? The knock sounded again. Scurrying to the door, she stared out the peephole and saw Stefan standing impatiently.

She immediately flung open the door. "What are you doing here?"

"Good evening to you, too," he said, walking inside and closing the door behind him. "Did you enjoy your time with Lafitte?"

"Not particularly," she said "I mean, he was nice enough and he definitely has an interesting backstory."

"Eve," he said, and she noticed he was clenching his jaw.

"And he wasn't surrounded by two beautiful women vying for his attention and willing to do anything to marry him."

"I didn't invite either of those women," he said.

"Either would be perfect for *the job*," she said, crossing her arms over chest.

"I'm not marrying either of those women," he said.

"How can you be sure?"

"Because I will make the ultimate decision and I refuse to give up my relationship with you for a wife I don't love."

Eve blinked. She hadn't expected that. "This thing between us is crazy," she said. "Pure crazy."

He pulled her into his arms. "I can't disagree, but I just found you and I'm not giving you up."

His words made her heart turn over at the same time that she knew she couldn't be what he ultimately needed. "You have duties. I can't be your princess."

"Shut up," he said. "Just for tonight," he asked more than ordered. "Shut up and let me make love to you."

Eve did, and Stefan took her to the top of the world, but when she awakened, she was alone. She tried not to overthink her relationship with him, but there was a part of her that hated the fact that they had to do everything in secret. They couldn't even eat a meal together because a photog would take pictures and draw conclusions. In this case, the conclusion would be correct.

She wondered if Stefan should be choosing a wife, a woman who could meet his needs as a friend, lover and a representative of Chantaine. She worried if such a combination of a woman existed. In quiet moments, she feared that woman did and would steal Stefan's heart. But how could his heart be stolen if it didn't truly belong to her?

Shut up, she told herself. *Just for this short time, let yourself love him....*

Three mornings later, she awakened to the sight of him pacing in front of her. He had persuaded her to stay the night in his quarters.

"Repeat that," he said, then stopped dead just in front of his bed. "It's not possible," he said after several moments. "It's *not* possible."

He began to pace again, dressed in pajama bottoms and nothing else. "I always used protection."

Eve blinked. *Whoa. Protection?*

"I demand a DNA test," Stefan said and then listened for another moment. "What do you mean there's already been a DNA test? How is that possible? I want a second one, and I want it done by the best labs in existence. We'll talk later," he said and then turned off his phone, staring blankly at the wall.

Moments later, he turned and met her gaze. "I assume you heard the conversation," he said.

"I heard the words *protection* and *DNA test*," she said, pulling the sheet over her as she sat up in bed. "Kinda an explosive combination," she said with a giggle bubbling from her throat.

He glared at her in astonishment.

"Sorry," she said, but another giggle escaped. She slapped her hand over her mouth, ripped the sheet loose and got out of bed. "I really am sorry. I'm nervous. That's why I'm reacting this way. Who is the child? Who is the mother?"

"The mother is Maja, the model I dated a couple years ago. Days after we broke off our relationship, she hooked up with that French billionaire. According to the press, he was the father of her child." He paused a took a half breath. "A daughter named Stephenia. She's not quite two."

Eve's heart twisted in sympathy. "Oh, she's just a baby. Why are they calling you now?"

"Maja and her husband died in a speed-boating accident," he said. "Maja didn't leave a proper guardian in her will. She left only a confidential note that I was the baby's father. Maja's husband never put the baby in his will."

"Oh, no," Eve said, shaking her head. "That poor child. You must bring her here immediately."

Stefan stared at her in disbelief. "I don't even know if she's truly my child. I need to hear the DNA confirmation—"

"But it sounds like they've already done a DNA test," Eve said.

"One," Stefan said. "For something this important, I insist on a confirmation. Plus, I need to consider what's best for the child and the royal family. In the past, the advisers have always insisted that an illegitimate child be raised away from the palace."

Eve dropped her jaw. "You must be joking. You're going to have a toddler raised by a nanny in Timbuktu so she doesn't tarnish the Devereaux name?"

"You have no right to accuse or criticize. There's been no decision made," he said.

"This isn't about accusing or criticizing. This is about doing what's right. Figure it out yourself, Your Royal Highly *Father*ness." She dropped her sheet and went to pull on her clothes.

"Eve," he said as she buttoned her shirt.

She met his gaze and saw a world of torment in his eyes.

"I'm not prepared to be a father," he said.

"Most men aren't," she said. "The difference is you have a whole crew of advisers and you can hire a couple nannies."

"And you?"

She frowned at him in confusion. "How would this change my feelings for you?"

"I don't know. You tell me," he said.

"The only way this would change my feelings is if you neglected or abandoned your child. And I don't think you're capable of either of those."

"This will be a PR nightmare. The high-ranking officials who have lobbied against me will be cheering," he said, raking his fingers through his hair.

"Or not," she said.

"What do you mean?" he asked.

"A few pics of you with the new little princess and anyone who criticizes you will be regarded as a bully," she said. "Just a warning, though. The pics will be easy.

Being a father is going to be the tough part." Taking in the shocked expression on his face, she moved closer and touched his hand. "I think you have the right stuff," she said.

He gave a short laugh without humor. "Me?"

"Yes, you. You know the kind of father you *don't* want to be. Maybe that will point you in the direction of the father you *do* want to be."

Chapter Nine

Stefan checked his watch for the tenth time in five minutes. The plane carrying his daughter had landed, and she would arrive shortly. The plan was for Stephenia to be brought to his quarters. He glanced at the time again and paced his office.

A moment later, his phone vibrated with a text message. The limo carrying his daughter was approaching the palace. Unable to wait a moment longer, he swept out of the office and descended two flights of stairs. Nodding absently to the staff he saw along the way, he came to a stop in the lobby.

Taking a deep breath, he waited for what felt like an eternity. The front door opened and one of his security staff escorted in a very young woman holding a tiny girl with a head full of dark ringlets and her thumb securely fastened into her mouth. Her eyes were wide as she cautiously surveyed her surroundings.

"Your Highness," the guard said with a bow.

"Thank you," Stefan said and moved closer.

"This is Hilda. She has been Stephenia's caretaker for the last two months," the guard said.

"Hello, Hilda," Stefan said to the young woman.

"Thank you, Your Highness," she said, and then she jostled Stephenia. "Stephie," she whispered. "This is your daddy. Say hello."

Stephenia looked at him then buried her head in Hilda's shoulder.

"She's a little shy and tired," Hilda said, giving Stephenia another nudge. "Come on, baby. This is your daddy," she said, then moved as if she planned to place Stephenia into Stefan's arms.

Stefan froze.

Stephenia let out a blood-curdling yell of terror.

Stefan lifted his hand. "Perhaps she'd like something to eat and a nap. One of the staff can take you both to the nursery."

As the child continued to scream down the hallway, Stefan wondered what in hell he'd been thinking. This baby knew nothing of him. When she looked at him, she was frightened, and rightfully so. He didn't know what to do with a two-year-old little girl. When he'd first seen her, she'd looked so innocent, so angelic. She looked like she'd needed to be protected and he'd been determined to protect her.

When she'd opened her mouth, however, he'd wondered if she was an alien. Part of him *still* wondered. How could anything so small produce such a loud, horrendous noise?

He shook his head. Now he understood why his father and predecessors had kept their illegitimate children off-site. Hell, if all children shrieked like that, it was a wonder his parents had allowed any children to grow up in the palace. Of course, he'd had a slew of nannies to take care of him before he'd been shipped off to boarding school.

Eve had painted a lovely visual of possibilities of Stefan with his new daughter, but as her screams vibrated off the marble floors, he wondered why his daughter would be willing to let him hold her, let alone take a picture with her. At this point, Stefan suspected it would be years before that happened.

"She's a screamer," Stefan announced to Eve. "My daughter is a screamer."

Eve bit her lip to keep from laughing. Stefan was perplexed. He also clearly had little experience with toddlers. "Most toddlers scream," she said, rubbing his back in a soothing motion.

"She screamed when she thought I was going to hold her," he confessed. "It wasn't a good first meeting."

"Well, she'd just flown halfway across Europe to an unfamiliar place. Her mother is nowhere in sight. I'm sure she was tired and frightened. No one is at their best when they're frightened. You have to give it a second try. Actually, since she's your daughter, you have to give it infinite tries."

"I'm giving it another try in a few minutes. Would you join me?" he asked.

Surprised, she studied him, then nodded. "Sure. What's the plan?"

He gave her a blank look. "We'll go to the nursery."

"Okay," she said, then clapped her hands together. "This is going to go better than the first meeting. I can feel it."

Moments later they entered the nursery where Stephenia was holding a blanket and sucking her thumb as she pushed on a playboard with a spinner, a noisy flashing button and other features fascinating to a two-year-old. Hilda sat on the other side of the room, overseeing the tyke.

Both Stephenia and Hilda looked up at the same time. The nanny stood. "Your Highness."

Stephenia shot a hard glance at Stefan, then Eve, then back at Stefan.

Stalemate, Eve thought, and then moved toward the play area and sat down. She pulled off her hat and put it beside her as she picked up a book. Then she started to read a book. She read the first page, then turned it. Seconds later, Stephenia wandered closer, and Eve felt the toddler looking over her shoulder. Eve turned another page and Stephenia sat down next to her, her blanket still tossed over her shoulder, her thumb firmly in her mouth.

As Eve continued to read, Stephenia leaned against her. Eve read the rest of the book, and Stephenia sat for a moment. Then she reached for Eve's Stetson and placed it on her little head.

Eve smiled. "Are you a little cowgirl?" she asked.

Stephenia looked away shyly.

Stefan moved closer and Stephenia's eyes rounded. Glancing up at him, she stiffened. Her lower lip puckered out and her face crumpled. She began to scream and cry.

Meeting Eve's gaze, he shrugged and turned away. Eve reached for her hat and her hand slid over Stephenia's forehead. She frowned. The child was hot, too hot. "I think she might have a fever," Eve said, slipping her hand over the toddler's head again. Stephenia clutched the hat and screamed louder.

"What?" Stefan asked, turning back around.

"I hadn't noticed," Hilda said, and then wrung her hands. "With all the change and excitement…"

"I'll arrange for the royal doctor immediately. Please stay with Stephenia," he said to Eve, then left the room.

"You don't feel good, do you, sweetie?" Eve said, pulling the toddler into her lap. "Here, you can borrow the hat. What hurts, darlin'?"

Stephenia continued to moan and occasionally sob at a lower volume.

"I'm not sure I'm the best person for this job," Hilda said. "I was just an assistant until the last few weeks, and I missed her fever. I think I should resign immediately."

"Oh, no," Eve said, her stomach twisting for Stephenia. "She's been through so much change. Please give it a little time."

"But this island is so isolated and I have no friends or family here," Hilda said.

"It's a beautiful island and not as isolated as you think. Wait a little bit before you make a decision. After things get more settled, you'll have another nanny working with you."

"But ever since we arrived here, she cries with me, too," Hilda said.

"Perfectly understandable if she's sick," Eve said, stroking Stephenia's hair and trying to comfort her.

Hilda looked at the toddler doubtfully. "We'll see," she said.

The door opened and a staff member poked her head through the door. "The doctor is here to see the baby."

Within twenty screaming minutes, the doctor diagnosed Stephenia with an ear infection and administered a first dose of antibiotics. Tired out by the examination and her fit of pain and fear, Stephenia fell asleep in Hilda's arms.

Stefan and Eve returned to his quarters. They sank onto the sofa together.

"That was exhausting," Stefan said. "I can't say it was better than yesterday."

"At least you have an explanation for her behavior," she said. "I bet you'd be cranky, too, if you had an earache."

"Can't deny that," he said, raking his hand through his hair. "Is it always going to be like this? When will she ever be more calm?"

Eve patted his hand. "Calm will come and go. A toddler is like the weather, sunshine one moment and stormy the next."

"How do you know this?"

"I babysat children from infants to ten-year-olds," she said. "Didn't you?" she asked, tongue in cheek.

"I can't say I did any official babysitting, but I have five younger siblings," he said. "None of them were screamers."

"That you know of," she said. "Maybe you weren't around during the screaming stage."

"Eve, what in hell am I going to do with this child?"

"Love her," she said. "She'll eventually come around."

"When she's twenty?" he asked in a dry tone.

"Oh, no, by then you'll drop at least a hundred IQ points, or so I hear," she said.

Stefan groaned. "Good luck getting your hat back," he said.

Eve laughed, remembering the way Stephenia had clutched her Stetson with a death grip during her entire examination. "Maybe you'll get her one of her own."

"That can be arranged. How did you win her over so quickly?" he asked.

"It's not magic. You can sit on the floor and read a book, too. You're different for her. Your voice is deeper, you're taller and scary to her. You'll have a better chance of winning her over if you get down on her level."

"I can't remember a time when my mother or father sat on the floor with me," he said, stroking his chin thoughtfully.

"You said you're going to do things differently," she said.

He paused and nodded. "Perhaps," he said. "Why does this suddenly seem so much more difficult than improving Chantaine's economy?"

She lifted her hand to his cheek and smiled. "Trust me. This is going to be cake compared to adolescence."

Stefan groaned. "I can't think about that right now."

"You've met Stephenia, haven't you?" Bridget said, and then covered her mouth as she giggled inside the café where they were eating lunch. "God is just. Stefan got a screamer." She giggled again. "Serves him right. He makes all of us want to scream."

"Have you spent time with her?" Eve asked.

Bridget paused. "I've seen her," she said. "I can't deal with screaming children."

"She's a motherless baby, and she's your niece," Eve said.

Bridget pouted. "Oh, you're spoiling all my fun," she said. "I'll be a good aunty eventually. I just don't enjoy infants and toddlers for more than an hour at a time...except for Valentina's daughter. She was a dream. Stephenia is a nightmare," she said in a lowered voice, then waved her hand in a dismissive gesture. "Besides, you and I are having this lunch to discuss the children's charity event. I like the idea of a hard rock/rap party."

"And how does this include children?" Eve prompted.

Bridget frowned. "I didn't know we had to include them. I thought we were just supposed to make money for them."

Eve chuckled. "Both can be done. We could make a day of it. Sand castles at the beach during the day and a beach party at night for the adults."

Bridget thought about the idea for a moment. "I like that, but I also like the idea of auctioning children's artwork."

"That's doable. Get a good band and some appetizers...."

"Oh, it should be a four-course meal," Bridget said.

"Not at the beach. And you want to make money. If you could pull in some celebrity appearances, that would make it even more appealing."

Bridget's eyes lit up. "Stefan and his first appearance with Stephenia."

Eve bit her lip, thinking about how difficult the current situation between Stefan and his daughter was. "I'm not sure you should count on that."

Bridget sighed. "Surely we can get the screamer to stop screaming by then."

"I know you're having a tough time with Stefan right

now, but at least you have him," Eve said. "At least you have your brothers and sisters."

Bridget's smile faded. "You must miss your brother very much. Why haven't you been in touch since you both became adults?"

"I can't find him and I suspect that if I can't find him, he may not want to be found," Eve said. "My upbringing wasn't at all cushy. He had it rougher than I did." Eve took a deep breath and fought back a sudden sting of tears that caught her off guard. "I know you and Stefan are often at odds, but please don't forget how important he is to you and how important you are to him. And I don't mean you're just important because of the duties you're currently performing."

Bridget glanced down at her glass and slid her finger around the rim of it. "I know what you're saying. Even though he was horrid to Valentina, and it seemed he was upset because she'd left him with no help, the real reason he was upset was that he couldn't protect her. He would croak if anything happened to any of us." She glanced up at Eve. "I still think his temperament would improve vastly if he had a wife…or at least a lover."

Eve couldn't say a thing.

Stefan waited until his daughter's temperature returned to normal to approach her in the nursery. She still screamed when he entered. When he sat on the floor and read like Eve had, Stephenia sat on the opposite side of the room and watched him with terror on her face. It stabbed him in his heart to know that his daughter feared him so completely.

He took Eve with him late one afternoon to observe. Stephenia was far more interested in Eve than him. Eve had managed to swipe back her hat while Stephie slept one night. Stephie wanted it back.

His daughter walked toward Eve and pointed to her black Stetson. "You wanna borrow my hat?" Eve asked. "Can you say please?"

Stephie kept her thumb in her mouth and continued to point.

Eve adjusted her hat. "Gotta say please," she said. "What's up for reading tonight, Your Highlyness?"

"The Cat in the Hat," he said, then sat on the floor just as he had for the last four nights.

"Oooh, one of my favorites," Eve said, joining him on the floor and looking at the book as he read it.

A few pages later, Stephenia appeared by Eve's side and tugged at the hat. Eve shook her head. "Say please," she said to the toddler.

Stefan paused. Eve nodded. "Please continue."

Stefan did as she requested. Two pages later, Stephenia said, "Peas?"

Eve beamed and immediately transferred her hat to the toddler's head. "What a smart girl. I'm so proud of you."

Stephenia gave a shy smile as the hat covered her down past her nose. "Peas," she said again.

"Good for you," Eve praised. "You like my hat, don't you?"

Stephenia pushed the hat back slightly so she could look at Eve. "Peas."

Eve clapped again. "Good girl."

Stefan's heart swelled in his chest at the same time he sensed this wasn't going to solve his problem. "So she knows how to say peas?" he asked.

Eve frowned at him. "It's a step forward."

"True, but we don't know if she's stopped screaming,"

he said. He reached toward the child, and she squeaked. "As I said."

Eve sighed. "True. Okay. I'm going to leave the room."

"Why?" he asked, fighting a terrible sense of panic.

"Because you and Stephenia need to learn to communicate," she said.

"I've been trying to do that with no success since you arrived here," he reminded her.

"True, and I really admire you for that," she said. "After I leave the room, I want you to whisper."

He glanced at her in surprise. "Are you serious?"

"Totally," she said as she left the room.

Stephenia stared after Eve, then turned her head and glanced warily at him.

"Yeah, I'm with you," he whispered. "I wish she would have stayed, too."

Stefan began to whisper the rest of *The Cat in the Hat* and one page before the end of the book, his daughter sat down next to him and leaned her head against his side.

He almost wept.

"Your Highness, more than ever," Tomas said. "You need a wife. With the scandal you've created by fathering an illegitimate child, the best solution for this PR debacle is for you to marry. Although," Tomas said, "I'm certain several of our top contenders will decline being considered."

"Because of Stephenia?" Stefan said more than asked.

Tomas shrugged. "At the level of your potential

mates, many of them would prefer not to deal with a stepchild."

"Then I wouldn't want that woman for my wife," Stefan said in a cold voice.

The senior adviser fidgeted. "Of course, sir. My interest, all of our interest, is only for the best for Chantaine—and you."

Stefan heard the order of priority. Chantaine first. Him second...or last. He'd always accepted it before. Now he had more to consider. Now he had Stephenia. "I have no intention of taking a wife at the moment. I'm forming a relationship with a daughter whom I didn't even know existed. In my personal relationships, my priority is helping Stephenia feel safe and secure and guiding my sisters and brothers into a closer familial relationship. That was neglected by my parents and the advisers. I'm determined to repair it."

Tomas looked cranky. "You and your siblings were provided with the best education possible. How were we to know that you needed some sort of sibling bond? None of your predecessors expressed such a need. Your father had little affection for his brother."

"I'm not my father," Stefan said.

The adviser met his gaze for a long moment, then looked away. "Your father had a different policy regarding illegitimate children," he muttered.

"Explain that," Stefan said.

Tomas shook his head. "It's nothing," he said. "Just a backup plan that was never necessary, thank God."

Stefan was half tempted to ask a few more questions about the backup plan, but he had no interest in further engaging the chief adviser. "I'm glad you understand my priorities."

"Yes, Your Highness, but soon you will need to take a wife."

"First things first," Stefan said crisply. "I am, however, taking recommendations for a nanny."

Tomas blinked, then furrowed his brow. "I'll make inquiries," he said. "I am happy to serve. There have been rumors, sir, that the child is—" Tomas coughed "—a bit vocal."

Stefan chuckled. "*Vocal* isn't an adequate term. She's a screamer, but we're working with her. Funny thing. When you whisper to her, she usually gets quiet."

The adviser turned solemn. "Congratulations, sir. If you have learned the secret of quieting a female, then you have learned the secret to peace."

Stefan shook his head. "I want my daughter to feel loved and secure. I haven't learned the secret to achieving that yet."

Tomas slowly nodded. "Your father would have never voiced such a concern. You are very different from him."

"I'll take that as a compliment," Stefan said.

The following day, Stefan and Stephenia took a field trip to the barns.

"I'm not sure this is a good idea," Eve said as she met them.

Her thumb stuck firmly in her mouth and her blanket clasped in her hand, Stefan's daughter stared wide-eyed in the soft daylight. She glanced at Eve, then stared at the black Stetson Eve had retrieved for the fifth time. Stephenia pulled her thumb from her mouth and pointed at Eve's hat. "Peas."

Eve glared at Stefan as she pulled her hat from her head. "We must get her a hat."

"I gave her a white one. She prefers yours," he said, carefully placing Eve's hat onto his daughter's head. Stephenia gave a Mona Lisa smile, and he wondered just how much his little daughter knew she was manipulating the adults.

"Yeah, yeah," Eve said. "Well, you know the routine. Please tell the nanny to collect my hat tonight when Stephie falls asleep."

"Of course," he said. "Are we going to introduce her to Black?"

"No way," she said. "Are you trying to terrify her for life?"

"Black would protect her," he said.

"After he frightened her to death," she said. "Gus. Gus is our man. He's a true gentleman," she said, then walked toward the gelding's stall. "Hey, handsome," she said, and the gelding immediately came to the stall door, nodding.

"I have someone I want you to meet. Be the sweetheart you are," she whispered, then motioned for Stefan to come closer.

"Isn't he gorgeous?" she said to Stephie. "He's so soft. His hair. His ears. Look at his ears, Stephie."

Stephie stared at the horse for a long moment, then waved her hand toward him.

"You want to touch him?" Stefan asked her and gently guided her hand against his neck. "Soft?"

She lifted her hand higher, and he guided her hand gently over Gus's ears. "Oooh," she said.

He smiled at the cooing sound and met Eve's gaze. "I think she likes him."

"Yeah, I think she does," she said, then watched as Stephenia slid her hand lower to Gus's nose.

The horse flared his nostrils and snorted, startling the child.

Eve laughed. "He made a funny sound, didn't he?"

Stephenia looked uncertain for a moment, then started to giggle.

Stefan stood stock-still. This was the first time he'd heard his daughter laugh. He wondered if he would breathe normally again.

Eve stroked Gus's nose and he snorted again.

Stephenia laughed louder, a belly laugh that echoed throughout the barn.

"One more time," Eve said, stroking Gus's nose again. He snorted.

Stephenia shrieked and laughed.

Stefan looked at Eve. "Is there any way we can record Gus's snort?"

"I think we should work on it. We should definitely work on it," she said.

"Would you join us for lunch?" he asked.

Touched by his invitation, she felt her heart twist and tighten. "Are you sure you shouldn't keep this just between the two of you?"

"Very sure," he said with just a hint of desperation in his eyes.

Eve gave into her sympathy. "Okay. Thank you very much. Lead on."

They were, at first, supposed to eat at a table in Stefan's quarters. Eve suggested a blanket on the floor.

"Picnic," she said. "Afterward, you can shake off the blanket and throw it in the washing machine. No fuss. No muss." She paused a half beat. "Well, I guess you won't be washing it, but a blanket picnic will make it less stressful for everyone."

Moments later, they were served food on the blanket.

Still wearing Eve's hat, Stephenia picked up her food from a tray on the blanket. "Umm," she said as she tasted chicken, mango and avocado.

"She's not a fussy eater," Eve said. "That's a good thing."

Stefan nodded as he took a bite of his club sandwich. "I want to thank you for the advice you gave me to whisper," he said. "It works most of the time."

"You might also want to give music a try," she said. "You would have to experiment to find out what kind she likes, but I'm betting your girl likes music."

Stefan glanced at his daughter as she continued to happily stuff her mouth with food from her tray. "You think so?"

"Oh, yeah. Just hope it isn't rap," she said with a twinge of amusement in her voice.

"You're enjoying this a bit too much," he said.

"You need to remember that before I met you, I thought you were the most arrogant man in the world," she said. "You've now been humbled by a human being who weighs less than thirty pounds."

"I'm not humbled," he said. "Stephenia and I are in the process of negotiations."

She couldn't hold back a laugh. "And who is winning this negotiation?"

He shot her a glance that somehow combined extreme sexiness and amusement. "It's a series of negotiations, and I will ultimately win."

"Yeah, I'll remember that," she said. "If you and I are still talking when she's a teenager, I definitely want to hear you say those words again."

"You and I *will* be talking when she's a teenager," Stefan said. "And I *will* ultimately win."

"We'll see," she said.

He shot her a look of irritation. "You shouldn't question me when I'm certain."

"Just being honest. Do you really want me not to be?" she asked.

He paused. "No," he said. "I need to see you tonight. After eight," he said.

Chapter Ten

Stefan was in his office with the minister of…something. *Energy,* he reminded himself, which was an important minister, but Stefan was distracted by the chorus of feminine laughter filtering through the cracked window to his office. He strained to catch a glimpse out the window.

Is that Bridget? Phillipa? He couldn't quite make out the other adult female until he saw the black Stetson. Eve. The swing was soaring and he could hear Stephenia cackle with joy. He smiled. His daughter's laughter was a sound that should be bottled. He was certain it had the potential to cure diseases and solve world peace.

"Your Highness," the minister prodded. "Are you following my plan?"

Stefan slid his hand over his face and shook his head. "I apologize, Charles. I'm distracted," he said, rising to reluctantly close the window. "Would you mind emailing me your notes? Perhaps another modality might help," he said wryly.

"Not at all, sir," the minister of energy said. "I have a young one myself. Amazing how they can wear you out in an hour. My wife is my lifesaver. I don't know how you do it."

"It takes a village," Stefan muttered. "But we're coming along. Stephenia is adjusting."

"And are you, sir?" Charles Redmond asked. "Forgive me for saying so, but many are concerned for you."

Stefan wrinkled his brow. "Why? I'm healthy and responsible."

Charles paused, sliding his hand over his receding hairline. "But a wife could make things so much easier for you. Have you given consideration to getting married?"

Stefan clenched his jaw for a second, then gave the man the benefit of the doubt. "I will eventually marry, but I think it would be wrong for me to rush into such an important partnership when I've just learned that I have a daughter. First things first. I will make sure Stephenia feels secure in her new home. Does that not make sense to you?"

"When you put it that way Your Highness, it does," Charles said.

Stefan wondered how many different ways he needed to put it since he'd said the same to countless advisers and ministers during the last couple of weeks. "Thank you for your concern and confidence in me," Stefan said. "I count on it."

Charles stood straighter. "Of course, sir. I have the utmost confidence in you."

"Thank you. I will have to invite you and your wife to dinner with your children," Stefan said.

Charles looked momentarily horrified. "Oh, thank you very much sir, but my children are not mature enough for a state dinner."

"I was thinking of something more casual. Perhaps you and your wife could share some of your tips," Stefan said.

"We would be honored," Charles said, then nodded his head. "Thank you again, sir. I'll get those notes to you directly."

"Thank you, Charles," Stefan said, then stood, signaling the minister to leave. As soon as Charles left, Stefan punched the extension for the royal public relations representative.

The representative immediately answered his phone. "Yes, Your Royal Highness. How may I serve you?"

Stefan felt a prickle of irritation. He'd asked the staff to change the way they addressed him to "How can I help you?" Some, however, refused to make the change.

"I want you to send a press release informing that I am enjoying my developing relationship with my daughter, Stephenia. My personal focus is on helping Stephenia to feel safe and secure in her new environment. After I am certain she has adjusted, I will be open to finding a woman who will be a mother to Stephenia, a wife to me and a princess to Chantaine. I appreciate all the support of my country during this exciting time of change."

Dead silence followed. "You're saying you won't take a wife right now."

"I'm saying I have other priorities at the moment," Stefan said. "I want you to send the release immediately."

"But, sir, Chantaine and half the world are waiting

to hear that you have found the right woman and are ready to marry," the PR representative protested.

"They need to get off the edge of their seats," Stefan said.

"But, sir—"

"This isn't a request," Stefan said firmly.

Another silence followed.

"Yes, sir," the representative said.

"Please email the announcement to me for final approval," Stefan said. "Thank you for your responsiveness. I appreciate it very much. Good day," he said, then hung up.

Loosening his tie, he stood and walked toward the window, opening it more as he watched his sisters and Eve play with Stephenia. The richness of the moment filled him up inside. His siblings were so often at odds with each other. Could they possibly come together over his surprise daughter? Hearing another peal of laughter, he smiled and decided to join them.

As he approached the trio of women surrounding Stephenia on the swing, he wished he had a camera to save this moment forever. His daughter was laughing as his sisters and Eve took turns pushing her in the swing.

"She really is irresistible when she's not screaming," Bridget said.

"I'm sure you were quite irresistible when you were a screaming toddler," Phillipa shot back to Bridget.

"How do you know I was a screamer?" Bridget said.

"Because Nanny used to put plugs in my ears whenever you came around," Phillipa said.

"You're making that up," Bridget said.

"I am not," Phillipa protested.

"We all had a screaming stage," Eve intervened. "Some are just louder and more shrill than others. Maybe Stephenia wouldn't have such a delicious laugh if she weren't also a screamer."

"Oh, I never thought of that," Bridget said.

Stephenia let out a full laugh.

Phillipa laughed in returned. "Oh, I think I would push this swing all night for that sound."

"Is that an offer?" Stefan asked.

All three women stared at him in surprise. Stephenia was still gleefully swinging.

"I thought you were stuck in meetings," Bridget said.

"I was, but the four of you distracted me," he said, unable to keep his lips from twitching.

Phillipa frowned. "How could we possibly distract you?"

"Your window was open, wasn't it?" Eve asked.

He met her gaze and something inside him eased. "Yes, it was. I scrapped the meeting and asked for an email summary."

"Good for you," Bridget said. "If there were a bigger swing, I would offer to push you, too."

"That's okay," Stefan said, sliding a sideways glance at Eve.

"I was thinking, however, that I would love to take her on brief public outings with me. You know the people of Chantaine would love to get a peek at her, and she is gorgeous. When she's not screaming," Bridget added.

"Not yet," Stefan said without missing a beat.

"I thought I could take her to the zoo when I visit France next week. Fredericka is dying to see her," Phillipa said.

"If you dare let her go," Bridget said, clearly peeved.

"She's not going anywhere," Stefan said. "Although I can't tell you how delighted I am that you're both enjoying her. Stephenia needs to get used to her environment and current routine. I want us to become familiar to her so she feels safe. We need to protect her during this time of adjustment and I will be very grateful to you for any time you choose to spend with her," he said, then gave his daughter's swing a push.

Bridget and Phillipa stared at him as if he'd grown an extra head. Then their gazes softened.

"When you put it that way..." Bridget said. "I would love to take her on Thursday afternoons."

"Tuesdays for me," Phillipa said. "Unless you need someone to rock her to sleep occasionally. I could read her books."

Stephenia's gaze locked on Stefan. "Book," she said. "Book."

Stefan heard Eve's throaty laugh and the combination of that sound with that of his daughter's gaze made him feel as if he was standing on Mt. Kilimanjaro.

"I think Daddy's been doing a lot of reading," Eve said.

Bridget's eyes turned shiny with emotion. "Oh, Stefan, you're going to be a good father. Much better than our father was."

"I like to believe he did the best he could," Stefan said. "I also like to believe that we can all do better."

Eve met his gaze, and Stefan was scored with the instinct to take her hand and pull her closer to him. To slide his arm around her and feel her against him. It would have been the right thing to do. His duty snapped through him like a strong static shock and he restrained the urge. Barely.

"You made my day. All of you," he said, then kissed his daughter on the top of her head. He exchanged a glance with Eve that lasted longer than it should, then forced himself to turn and walk away.

Later that night after they'd made love, Eve turned to Stefan. "Let's go for a ride," she said.

"Now?" he asked, knowing it was close to midnight.

"What? Is it too late for you? Are you too old to go out this late?" she challenged.

"No," he said, sitting up in bed. "But why do you want to go now?"

She sighed. "Because I want to be with you somewhere besides your bed," she said, staring up at the ceiling. "It's hard being a secret," she said in a low voice.

"I hate it, too," he said. "Today, when I saw you with Stephenia and my sisters, I wanted to pull you into my arms so much I hurt with it."

She slid her hand over his chest, making his heart beat faster. "I understand why we need to keep our relationship secret, but—" She groaned. "Sometimes it's hard."

"It is," he agreed, pulling her against him, relishing the sensation of her breasts against his bare skin and the sight of her wavy hair hiding one of her eyes.

"We could take a quick trip to Paris," he said. "I could arrange for a private dinner, then we could take a walk at night when the photogs aren't watching."

"When are the photogs *not* watching?" she asked.

True, he thought. *Too true.* But Eve had become like oxygen to him. He needed her in order to feel whole.

The realization shook him. Stefan stared at her and felt a kick that reverberated throughout him. She was the first woman who'd ever made him feel this way. What the hell was he going to do about it?

As much as Stefan had always hated his father's playboy-with-the-yacht image, he could see the benefit of the vessel. The yacht could provide a day of needed escape from the prying eyes of the grounded photogs in Chantaine. A perfect getaway.

"Meet me in my quarters in fifteen minutes," Stefan told Eve at 5:00 a.m. from his cell phone.

"What?" she said, her voice groggy with sleep. "It's not even dawn."

"Exactly. My yacht is taking us out for the day," he said.

A pause followed. "That sounds fabulous, but I think you've forgotten that you're not dealing with a countess or a princess. You're dealing with a working girl and I have things to do today…Your Highness," she added, clearly as an afterthought.

"Surely you can reschedule or have your assistant handle your duties for the day. What if you were ill?"

"Exactly. What if I were sick?" she retorted. "I need to save my sick days for when I'm sick. I'm certain my employer wouldn't appreciate me shirking my duties for a yacht trip."

"In this case, I can tell you that your employer most certainly wants you to meet with him on his yacht."

"That almost sounds official," she said.

She sighed. "But I know it's not. I also know I would love to be with you whether we're on a yacht or in a canoe. Give me ten extra minutes," she said.

"I'll give you fifteen. A driver will pick you up."

An hour later, they were watching the sunrise from the yacht as they sailed away from the harbor.

"It's beautiful, isn't it?" she said, leaning her shower-dampened head against his shoulder.

He sifted his fingers through her hair. "Yes, you are," he said and took her mouth in a kiss.

She gave a low chuckle. "I was talking about the view."

"So was I," he said and kissed her again. He could get addicted to kissing Eve. Every time his mouth took hers, he tasted a combination of sensuality, desire, honesty and…love? Could it possibly be?

Determined not to question such a pleasurable moment, he slid his arm around her waist and drank in the sunrise with her.

"The last time I saw a sunrise this beautiful was after a foal was born. It had been a long night and it wasn't an easy delivery, but both the mom and baby survived. After that long dark night, the sunrise was glorious," she said and looked up at him. "What about you? When was the last time you saw a sunrise this beautiful?" she asked.

"Never," he said. "Never saw one with you."

She met his gaze then narrowed his eyes. "Be careful. I might start to think you really care for me. Or that you're a master seducer. Neither of those would be good."

"What if one were true?" he asked.

Her gaze turned vulnerable. "Like I said. Neither would be good." She closed her eyes for a moment as if to push away ugly doubts, then crossed her arms over herself.

In protection, he realized. Frustration slid through him. *He* wanted to protect her.

"After all this rushing around, I'm starving. Are you going to feed me?" she asked.

"Whatever you want," he said. "Including American bacon. I requested it especially for you."

"Oh, now I know you want me for your slave," she said. "Bacon."

"If that's all it takes," he said.

"I was joking," she said.

"Damn," he muttered, then waved for one of the staff.

After a substantial breakfast, Stefan taught Eve to steer the yacht. They anchored in a private, deserted cove and dove into the cool, azure water.

With her hair slicked back and water clinging to her dark eyelashes, Eve wrapped her legs around him for warmth in the water. "This is cold."

"You're used to wimpy Texas water holes," he said, sliding his hands over her silky skin.

"They're not wimpy," she protested. "But they're warmer than this."

"Our ocean is usually warm and the palace pool is always warm," he said.

"I wouldn't know," she teased. "That's off-limits for me since I'm not a Your Highlyness."

He gave her a soft pinch and she squealed. "What was that for?"

"I wonder how you would react if someone called you 'Your Highlyness'," he said.

"I have no fear of that," she said. "Because no one ever would. I'm a working girl, remember."

"Hmm," he said, his mind moving in directions he'd never thought possible. He shook his head and reined in his thoughts. "Let's go back to the deck. Your lips are turning blue."

They spent the entire day rotating between water, shade and sun. Stefan couldn't remember a day when he'd felt more free. As the sun set, he knew their time together would end soon. He had his duties, and she had hers.

They toasted with champagne and dined on fish and vegetables. He could tell Eve enjoyed the meal by the approving sounds she made.

He smiled. "Like the food?"

"Delicious," she said. "I love fish, but I'm usually so busy I just grab a sandwich."

"Then you're too busy," he said as they moved from the table to cushioned bench. "The parade is over. You can relax now."

"Black and some of the others are competing soon. I have to stay on top of them. When they perform well, you look good. I'm determined to make you look good," she said.

"And that is one of the many things I like about you, Eve Jackson," he said, lifting his hand to push a strand of her hair from her face. He couldn't quite read her expression, but he sure as hell wanted to know what was going on inside her. "Three wishes," he said. "If you could have three wishes, what would they be? And they can't include world peace or a cure for killer diseases."

"Well, darn, you took my first two. I have my dream job. I'm on the water on this incredible day with an incredible man. What else could I possibly want?" she asked. When he continued to wait for an answer, she sighed and closed her eyes for a long moment. "I'd really like to see my brother again. I'd really like to know that he's all right." She finally opened her eyes and met his gaze. "And I'd like for you to be happy."

He made a mental note of her brother, but was

surprised when she'd mentioned his happiness. "What makes you think I'm not happy?"

"Your Highlyness, you are a tortured soul," she said, gently poking her finger at his chest. "If you're not fighting the image your father left behind, then you're fighting your advisers about what you want to accomplish now and in the future. Your job is never done. Do you ever feel a sense of accomplishment?"

"I do today," he said. "I successfully kidnapped you and spent a day away from the compound."

"Do you really feel that way about the palace?" she asked. "Like it's a compound or prison? I can certainly see why you would."

"I have mixed feelings about the palace because I do a lot of work there. Although I'm protected from the press and prying eyes, it's not always easy to relax." Except with her, he thought. When Eve was close by, something inside him eased. "The sun is setting. We have a few more moments. No more talk about the compound, okay?"

She met his gaze and lifted her hands to cup his face. "Okay, Your Highlyness," she said and leaned closer to kiss him.

The next day at lunchtime, Bridget walked into Eve's office at the stable. Eve chuckled to herself. Princess Bridget was nothing if not predictable with her timing.

"Hellooooo?" Bridget called cheerily from the doorway and placed a cellophane-wrapped bag of foil candies onto her desk. "I brought chocolate this time instead of lunch since you didn't seem to enjoy the last lunch I brought."

"Good afternoon, Your Highness. How can I help you?" Eve asked.

"Oh, please drop the 'Your Highness.' You and I are friends. And I do have some juicy gossip about Stefan. I got it off the internet. Apparently Stefan went out on his yacht with a woman yesterday," she said and thrust the story and photo at Eve.

Eve's breath and heart stopped. The words blurred in front of her. The photo featured Stefan, shirtless, his head tilted back with a smile of delight on his face. Opposite him, a woman's feet and legs extended from beneath an umbrella.

"They only got a show of the woman's feet and legs up to the knees," Bridget said.

Eve curled her toes inside her boots. She cleared her throat. "Those cameras are amazing."

"Yes, they are, but it's a shame they couldn't have gotten a shot of the woman's face or even her body. All we've got now is this photograph of her feet and from the looks of it, she needs a pedicure," she said with a sniff.

Eve resolved to scrub her feet with a pumice stone and paint her toenails that evening. "It's hard to tell much detail from the photo," she said.

"True, it could just be a bad French pedicure. Either way, this is good and bad news," Bridget said.

"How is that?" Eve asked.

"It's good because Stefan is seeing a woman. It's bad because he's not seeing the woman I chose for him," Bridget said with a pout.

"Hmm," Eve said because she couldn't conjure another response.

Bridget sighed. "Well, I'll keep trying because I believe Stefan needs a wife even if he doesn't realize it. But that's not why I came to see you." She paused, staring at Eve for a moment. "You're sunburned, darling."

Eve bit her lip, thinking about all the time she'd spent on the yacht yesterday. "I've been training the horses outside a lot lately. Maybe that's it."

"You need to be more careful. Use more sunscreen. Always reapply," Bridget preached.

"Excellent advice," Eve said.

"The other reason I came is that I'm making a different appearance next week and I'd really appreciate it if you would come with me," Bridget said.

Curious, she watched Bridget almost fidget. "What kind of appearance?"

"I'm visiting disadvantaged teenage girls. I'm taking gently worn designer clothing and encouraging them to focus on bettering themselves," she said. "I hope it won't be a disaster."

"No. It's a great idea. I just wonder if it needs another element," she said.

"Such as what?" Bridget asked.

"An educational push. Are there scholarships available for these girls? Trade, academic…"

Bridget paused thoughtfully then smiled. "I like it. No, I love it. I'll talk to the educational minister right away."

"So what do you need me for?" Eve asked.

Bridget bit her lip. "Texas courage?"

Eve laughed. "You've got it."

Two nights later, Stefan invited her to dinner. Eve was torn about joining him after the internet article. She knew her relationship with Stefan needed to remain secret for both their sakes. A public outing of their affair would be devastating for the credibility of both of them.

Vacillating until the last moment, she left her apartment and sped down the stairs to the front door where Max waited for her.

"Ms. Jackson, I wasn't sure you were coming," he said.

"I wasn't sure, either," she muttered and strode toward the palace, thankful for the cleansing breeze that blew over her hot cheeks.

"Are you all right, ma'am?" he asked. "Is there something you need?"

Despite the fact that Max was trained to kill in more than fifty ways, he was a teddy bear. "I'm fine. Just a little tense tonight. Thank you."

"You're very welcome, ma'am. If you do need something, let me know," he said as they drew next to the palace door and he opened it for her.

"Thanks," she said, looking at Max. He was about the age her father would have been if he were still alive. She wondered what her life would have been like if she'd had a father like Max. "You're a good man. Good night."

She climbed the stairs to Stefan's suite, still filled with mixed feelings. She barely lifted her hand to knock and the door swung open. "Come in," Stefan said.

As soon as she stepped inside, he pulled her into his arms and whirled her around. A giddy sensation bubbled inside her. "What are you doing?" she asked breathlessly.

"It's been two long days since I've seen you. Too bloody long," he said, then took her mouth.

Her head immediately began to spin. "But the photog," she protested.

"What photog?" he asked, stopping.

"The one on the internet. Bridget showed me the article," she said.

He laughed. "Oh, that one. All they got were your feet."

"And you can be sure I scrubbed and painted my toenails right away," she said.

"I look forward to seeing them," he flirted.

"Stefan," she said, meeting his gaze. "Seriously, don't you think this was a little close? You and I agreed that we want our relationship to remain between just you and me."

He appeared to stifle a sigh. "Yes, we did. But what's the worst that could happen?"

She stared at him in disbelief. "Besides your losing credibility and being shamed because you're cavorting with staff? Or I could lose all respect for my work with horses. In fact, your entire stables could be called into question. That's all."

He raked his hand through his hair and his face lost its joy. "You're right," he said. "But I find myself straining against the secrecy. Tell me you didn't enjoy our time on the yacht," he said, sliding his hands over her shoulders.

"Of course I did, but I also don't want to cause you any pain or hardship. Your job is hard enough as it is," she said.

He slid his hands around the nape of her neck and pulled her toward him. "Are you always so sensible?"

"Not exactly," she drawled. "I got involved with you, didn't I?"

He kissed her and kissed her and they didn't have dinner until much, much later. After they dined, she rested on him, her head against his chest. Her body was still buzzing from their lovemaking.

"I've had nonstop meetings the last two days. That's why I haven't called. I think I've found another way to bring more business to Chantaine," he said. "Turns out there are jazz festival tours that draw fans from all over the globe. We just need to work on finding a discount airline to make tourist travel easier."

"I thought you didn't want to bring in too many tourists," she said.

He shrugged. "There's a balance I don't think we've reached yet. We need more employment, more opportunities for our people. I think we need to keep pushing. If necessary, we can eventually pull back."

"That sounds like a good plan," she said, but her mind bounced back to what he'd said earlier about allowing their relationship to become public. His remark had been uncharacteristically reckless. "I'm a little tired. I need to go to bed."

"I'd like you to stay here," he said.

That was the problem, she thought as her heart jumped. "I don't want to bump into your morning staff," she said with a wink and a smile. "I should go. Sweet dreams, Stefan."

The next morning, Eve's alarm awakened her way too early. She pushed the snooze button. Four times. Finally, she forced herself from bed and scrubbed the sleep from her eyes. She really was going to have to start taking a day off every week where she slept late and spent the day watching mindless TV.

Daylight seemed to be coming earlier and earlier each morning. Turning on the jets to the shower, she stripped from her nightgown, still sensitized by how Stefan had touched her and made love to her the night before.

His touch affected her in a primal way. The more she was with him, the more she wanted to be with him, the more she wanted to protect him and be protected by him. How crazy was that? It was totally irrational, she thought, as she stepped into the shower and willed the water to give her some good sense. She was no princess, no countess, no blue blood. She was a Texan hick done good by going to college, and then following her dream to make her living by working with horses. Her current job was a dream. Her affair with Stefan was insanity.

After she scrubbed herself thoroughly, she dried off and put on her terry-cloth robe. Her coffeemaker greeted her with the smell of a fresh pot. "Thank you very much," she said, then poured herself a cup. Splurging, she dumped in some cream and sweetener.

Hearing the thud of the newspaper against her door, she retrieved it, glancing at the headlines as she sipped her coffee. Unemployment. Hope for New Job Opportunities. Who Is Prince Stefan's Girlfriend?

Her heart sank to her feet, and her coffee cup shattered on the floor.

Chapter Eleven

For the next three days when Stefan texted Eve, inviting her to join him for dinner, she refused. Spotting her feet featured on the internet was one thing, but seeing a photograph of her feet on the front page of Chantaine's newspaper was a horse of a different color. Eve refused to endanger her or Stefan's reputation, and she was frankly surprised that he wasn't more upset about the publicity than he acted.

After taking Black for a ride, Eve settled the stallion in his stall with his new friend Cupcake, the hornless goat. She'd gradually introduced the two of them with complete supervision. At first Black had been curious. Then he'd ignored Cupcake. She'd just about given up on the match when she'd spied Black nuzzling the goat. Now they were best buds.

She heard a sound and glanced behind her to find Stefan carrying Stephenia in his arms. Her heart skipped over itself. "We're the search party sent to find you," Stefan said, walking toward Eve. "We've missed you."

Her chest tightened at the raw emotion she saw in his eyes. She'd missed them, too. "I just thought, after the newspaper article, it might be best if I were less visible."

"The Chantaine newspaper isn't known for their journalistic integrity," he said in a dry voice.

"I know, but I don't like being the cause of discussion and speculation about you," she said.

"There will always be speculation about me, even when there's no basis for it. I can't let that kind of speculation keep me from what's important to me," he said.

What's important to me... She hadn't intended to become so important to him and she sure hadn't intended for him and his family to become so important to her.

Stephenia pointed at Eve's hat. "Peas."

Allowing herself the distraction from her disturbing thoughts and emotions, she smiled and gave the toddler the hat. "You said the magic word."

"Speaking of magic, it looks like your idea for Black has worked well," Stefan said, glancing in the stall. "I've heard of goats settling down racehorses, but I wouldn't have thought it would work for Black."

"He was lonely," Eve said. "They're herding animals, so when they don't have anything to herd, it makes them edgy."

"Well, now that you're finished for the day, Stephenia and I would like you to join us for dinner," he said. "And we're not taking no for an answer," he added before she could form a refusal. "Right, Stephie?" he prompted, stepping closer to Eve.

The toddler lifted her arms for Eve to hold her, stealing her heart all over again. Eve took the child in her arms and drank in her sweet, clean scent. She cast a sideways glance at Stefan. "You're playing a little dirty."

"All's fair," he began.

Panicking at the possibility of hearing the rest of that quote from his mouth, *in love and war,* she interrupted. "Yeah, yeah, yeah. What's for dinner?" she asked, changing the subject as she carried Stephenia on her hip and turned out the lights.

"It's a surprise," he said and opened the door for her. The limo waiting a few yards away sprang to life and the driver opened the door. After a short drive, the car stopped at the side entrance of the palace and Stefan carried his daughter up to his quarters with Eve walking beside him.

"I don't trust her on these stairs yet. Marble is unforgiving," he said.

Eve felt an extra warmth curl through her at his growing protectiveness toward Stephenia. "This would be a good practice activity with the nanny or you when you're feeling extra patient. The advantage to letting her do some of her own walking and climbing is that it—"

"Wears her out," he finished for her as they entered his suite. "Yes, I'm learning that. She doesn't have as much energy for screaming that way."

Eve noticed the dining table was already set. She also noticed some other changes. "Gates? No collectibles on the coffee table?" She gave a mock gasp. "You childproofed your domain."

He shot her a darkly amused look. "I'm told it's temporary," he said as he set Stephenia down. "It will return to normal in two or three years if I'm lucky."

The toddler immediately went to a corner of the room, which held a toy box. She opened the box and began pulling out all of the toys. Eve chuckled to herself.

"You're enjoying this too bloody much, Eve," he said, sliding his hand through hers and tugging her toward him.

"Hard on your dignity to have a toddler, isn't it?" she said, and he stole a kiss before she could turn away. Stephenia was too engrossed with her toys to notice.

"I should warn you there won't be any candlelight during this dinner," he said.

"No problem," she said. "I can't wait to see how the new dad deals with the two-year-old and her food."

"For such a beautiful child, she can be a little savage," he said, clearly disconcerted. "I'll call for the staff to deliver the food."

Eve washed up and helped Stephenia do the same. By the time they returned to the dining area, the staff was serving the food. The scent of barbecued ribs filled the room.

Eve stared at Stefan in surprise as he waved her toward the table. "Are those really baby back ribs?" she asked, stunned.

"They really are. The chef extracted the recipe from your aunt. He said it required intense negotiations."

Eve chuckled. "I'm sure she swore him to secrecy," she said. "And then promised him she would come after him like a wounded animal if he didn't stick to the deal."

"You know her well," he said and held out his hands to Stephenia. "Come here little one. Time to eat."

Stephenia allowed him to place her in her high chair and surveyed her meal of carrots, Italian broccoli, apple slices and chopped up bites of meat. She picked up a carrot and shoved it into her mouth.

"She eats better when she feeds herself," he said in

a long-suffering voice. "But watching her can kill your appetite."

"I'm amazed that you're taking some meals with her," she said. "I didn't expect you would be the kind of father to—" She broke off when she realized she'd misjudged him. "I apologize for that. You don't deserve it. You barely found out you had a daughter and look how far you've already come."

"Never in a million years did I imagine that I would be a single parent with a toddler daughter. The advantage that I have is that my sisters will take part in raising her and I also have nannies. Stephenia and I won't eat all our meals together, but I plan to set aside several times during the week where she and I share meals. It's one more way for her to grow accustomed to me."

Stephenia lifted a piece of broccoli toward him.

"Thank you very much," he said and lifted the vegetable to his mouth and pretended to eat it. "Very good."

Stephenia beamed and stuffed an apple slice into her mouth.

Eve took her first bite of the ribs and moaned in pleasure. "Delicious. Wonderful. Fabulous."

Stefan shot her a sensual gaze. "Your tone of voice sounds remarkably similar to when I—"

Eve felt her face heat and shook her head "Okay. Little ears. She may not understand, but you better start practicing what you say in front of her because she will repeat it. Thank you again for the ribs."

"Do they help appease the homesickness?" he asked.

"Yes," she said. "They do and they're delicious. I'm very touched that you would go to such trouble for me."

"It wasn't that much trouble," Stefan said. "But I

would have hated to have to go through with my threat to pull the guillotine out of the dungeon if my chef couldn't get the recipe."

"Oh, you didn't," she said.

"Since the chef was successful, we'll never know, will we?"

Stephenia ate several more bites, then began to offer the rest of her food to both Eve and Stefan.

"I think this means she's done," Eve said.

"Bath time," he said and called for the nanny.

They leisurely enjoyed the rest of the meal and Eve updated Stefan on her progress with the horses. His phone beeped and he took the quick call. "Would you like to say good-night to Stephenia with me?" he asked.

"I'd love to," she said, then walked down the long hallway to the nursery. Stephenia's eyes were already drooping and her thumb was tucked firmly in her mouth.

Her gaze lit up as Stefan entered the room. "Book," she said, pointing her finger at him.

"Again?" he asked and took the child from the nanny. "Say good-night to Eve," he said.

Eve moved closer to give Stephie a kiss. Stephie surprised her by placing a wet kiss on her cheek. "Oh, what a cutie," she said. "Sweet dreams, darlin'," she said, and then backed away as Stefan sat in the rocking chair and read the book under a dim light.

His low voice was soothing and he rocked slowly as he stroked his daughter's head. Her heart twisted so tight inside her she could hardly breathe. He was being so tender with her. This moment was just for the two of them. Suddenly feeling as if she were intruding, she quietly backed out of the room.

Taking a deep breath, she closed her eyes and was stunned to feel her eyes damp with tears. She wondered why she was so emotional. Swiping her eyes, she thought back to her own childhood. Her father had never rocked her to sleep. Her father had never read a book to her. Her father had never been a *father* to her.

It all hit her at once. Seeing Stefan become a loving father so quickly showed her what kind of man he was underneath. She had already fallen in love with him, but—alarm shot through her. No, she told herself. Not the *L* word. Not with Stefan. Their relationship was impossible. He knew it. She knew it. How could this have happened?

Distressed, she turned blindly down the hallway. She needed to leave immediately. Turning the corner, she walked straight into a man. Chagrined, she patted his arm. "Oh, gosh, I'm so sorry. I wasn't looking where I was going. Are you okay?"

"I'm fine," the white-haired man said in a testy voice. "Are you staff? What are you doing on this floor?"

"I was invited to—" She stopped, realizing she didn't want to reveal more. "I was just leaving. Again I'm sorry."

"Just a moment," he said when she turned. "Do you know where Prince Stefan is? I'm trying to reach him about an urgent matter."

She felt an invisible barrier slide upward. It came out of nowhere. She wasn't sure she liked this man. "His Royal Highness is already taking care of urgent business," she said. "I'm certain he'll be available in fifteen or thirty minutes. If it's not a matter of utmost importance, then you should try to reach him again later."

He looked taken aback by her don't-mess-with-me

tone and lifted his chin. "Do you know to whom you're speaking? I am one of Prince Stefan's lead advisers, Tomas Gunter. I do not take orders from staff. Give me your name."

"My name is Eve Jackson," she said. "And I meant it when I said that Stefan is taking care of urgent business. Don't bother him."

Eve heard footsteps in the hallway coming toward them. Stefan rounded the corner, lifting his eyebrows in surprise as he approached them. "Good evening, Tomas. I'm surprised to see you here at this hour."

"Your Royal Highness, you know I wouldn't bother you if it weren't a matter of importance," the adviser said. "Your staff member here told me you were taking care of urgent business."

Stefan glanced at Eve and tossed her a questioning glance.

"Time for me to go," she said with a smile that looked more like a grimace and backed away. "Y'all don't stay up too late. Sweet dreams."

"Eve," Stefan called, not liking the look of panic she was trying to conceal.

"I'll catch you up on your stallion later," she said. "Really. G'night," she said and whirled away.

He looked after her and sighed. Something had happened to upset her. They'd been separated barely five minutes. What the hell could it have been? Stefan turned to Tomas and frowned. "What did you say to Ms. Jackson?"

"Nothing," the adviser said. "I told her I needed to talk to you, and I questioned her as to why she was on this floor. That *is* a security breach," he said defensively. "She just kept insisting that you were conducting urgent business, and that I wasn't to interrupt you. I found that impertinent, bordering on subordinate."

Stefan chuckled. "She was right. I was conducting urgent business. I was rocking my daughter to sleep."

Tomas stared at him with a blank expression on his face. "I don't know what to say, sir. I never dealt with this kind of thing from your father."

"You've just paid me a high compliment," Stefan said and walked toward his suite. He didn't appreciate Tomas interrupting his evening with Eve. He'd practically had to trick her into joining him and now she'd fled. "It's late. If you don't mind, could you reveal to me the pressing matter that brought you here tonight?"

The adviser shifted uncomfortably. "I think it's best if we speak in private."

Reluctant to let the man into his quarters, Stefan obliged the adviser. "I have another matter to address tonight. I would appreciate brevity."

"Of course, sir," the adviser said, and Stefan shut the door behind him.

Tomas locked his hands behind his back and began to pace. "Your Royal Highness, unfortunate rumors are being spread about you, and you must take action to nip them in the bud. The rumor is that you have become sexually involved with one of your staff. I don't need to tell you that this will reduce your effectiveness as Crown Prince of Chantaine. You've told me of your high aspirations to help your country, and this kind of tawdriness will do nothing to help you. In fact," he said, "it can only hurt you, the royal family and the entire country of Chantaine."

Eve spent the following day feeling emotionally tortured. She had done the stupid, stupid, stupid thing of falling in love with Stefan. From the beginning, they'd both known their relationship would be temporary, but she had not been able to turn herself away from him. In retrospect, her feelings for him had been like a runaway train and all she could do was hold on for dear life.

Now, big things were at stake, such as the future of Stefan's family legacy and his ability to help his country the way he needed to help them. Eve knew Stefan well enough that she understood his duty to his country ran deeper than his blood. He would do anything for the citizens of Chantaine, and she loved him for that devotion. She also knew that his feelings for her ran deeper than either she or he had expected. She couldn't allow him to be swayed by his feelings for her. They would pass.

Her stomach knotted at the thought. But she told herself it was the truth. There were women lined up around the world ready, willing and able to be Stefan's wife. Women far more refined and polished than she would ever be. She just didn't know how she could make him understand.

She heard the door to the barn open and stepped out of Gus's stall. She wondered if it was one of her apprentices. Eve was fortunate to have plenty of help taking care of Stefan's stables. She walked toward the barn entrance and stopped when she saw the backlit figure of the adviser she'd met last night.

"Mr. Gunter?"

"Yes, and you are Ms. Jackson, correct?" he said and sneezed into his elbow. He walked a few steps farther and sneezed again. "Excuse me. I'm allergic to horses, dogs, cats and hay."

She dipped her head. "We have a lot of hay and

horses around here. Are you looking for something in particular?"

"Yes," he said, sniffing. "I was looking for you. May we speak in private?"

Eve felt a nauseating sense of dread. She knew she didn't want to have this conversation. "Unless it concerns the horses, I'm not sure it's necessary," she said.

"It concerns the owner of the horses," the adviser said. "Please," he said. "I won't take much of your time."

The *please* got her. It usually did. "Okay. There's an office this way," she said and led the way.

She heard the adviser sneeze three times. "Would you prefer to talk somewhere else, outside of the barn where you'll be less miserable?" she asked.

"This is fine," he said. "Thank you, though, for your consideration." He closed the door behind him. "It's very rare that I would consider directly interfering in Prince Stefan's private life, but he's an exceptional man and I believe he has an exceptional future. I believe he can bring a new sense of hope and change to Chantaine. He's not content to operate the same way his father did. His Royal Highness is a workaholic. He has a passion for Chantaine. Because of that, I feel compelled to protect him from an—" He paused. "An impulsive decision that could prevent him from fulfilling what he believes is his destiny."

Eve took a breath. Mr. Gunter was only saying what she'd expected and in her heart of hearts, she agreed with him. "You're talking about the relationship Stefan and I share," she said.

"He believes he's in love with you," the adviser said bluntly.

"And you don't," she said.

Gunter sighed. "I must look at the big picture. As

lovely and caring as you are, you are still a commoner and an American," he said as if her nationality were a detriment.

Eve couldn't hold a stone face at the slur against her country. "What's wrong with being American?"

The adviser lifted his hands. "Nothing, but if Stefan chose to marry a commoner, it would be best if he married a woman from Chantaine.

"For a prince, marriage is about more than love. It's a way to seal ties with other countries, secure trade agreements."

"What you're saying is it's business," she said.

"In a way," he said.

"But what about Stefan's heart?" she asked. "Who's going to look after that? Will you? Can I count on you to make sure that he gets a woman who will love him, love Stephenia, ride horses with him, respect him, challenge him when necessary, make him laugh, make him relax, make him think?" She ran out of breath.

Gunter shot her a considering gaze. "You are more than I thought you would be," he said, then wrinkled his brow as he thought. He sneezed into his sleeve, then nodded to himself. "In the past, happiness has not been a primary consideration when choosing a wife. It didn't hurt if the woman was beautiful and intelligent, but in general, what she could bring to benefit Chantaine was considered more important. What you're saying is that Stefan's happiness should be considered. I agree and I will make it my mission to make sure that the prince achieves the best match possible and that includes a woman who will indeed love him and, as you say, make him laugh. You're an extraordinary woman, Ms. Jackson. I understand the prince's fascination with you."

She pushed her hair behind her ear. "No need for flattery. I'm going to need to leave Chantaine, aren't I?"

"I'm afraid so, ma'am," he said.

The realization slashed through her like a sharp knife, and pain twisted and thrust through her. She took a shallow breath and tried to think. Was this the right thing to do? Why did it feel wrong when her brain told her it was right? "I need to keep a commitment to Princess Bridget."

Gunter nodded. "Of course. Just try not to linger. A clean break will be easiest for all, including yourself."

"Not sure about that," she muttered.

"Thank you for meeting with me," he said, extending his hand. "I wish you every good thing in your future, and if there is anything I can do to assist you, please do call me."

With mixed feelings, she shook his hand and nodded. "I'm curious, sir. In your role as adviser, have you had to do this kind of thing often?"

"Don't quote me, but many times with Stefan's father. Never with Stefan. And never with such a high-quality individual as yourself. You made it difficult," he said and shook her hand. "Good luck, Ms. Jackson."

He turned and left, and Eve felt as if she'd cut out her heart and thrown it on the floor. Filled with confusion, she sank her head into her hands and tried to think of another way. Why did it have to be so hard for both of them? Why? she asked herself and her chest grew tight and her eyes burned with tears.

She loved Stefan. She had to do what was best for him. That meant leaving Chantaine.

That also meant she needed to get the horses in tiptop shape for the next stable master. In the meantime, she created a file of careful notes for each horse for her successor. She was determined to make the transition as seamless as possible. She reviewed the information with her assistants and spent extra time with them to ensure they understood what needed to be done for each horse.

She successfully avoided Stefan by burying herself in work at the stable, although she missed him and little Stephenia. Wednesday finally arrived and she dressed for the charity event with Princess Bridget.

Bridget picked her up in a limo. "I'm a little nervous," she said to Eve. "This is one of our disreputable neighborhoods. It's a bit dangerous," she said.

"I'm proud of you for stepping out of your comfort zone," Eve said.

Bridget widened her eyes at the compliment and lifted her chin. "Well, thank you. That's high praise coming from you."

Eve laughed. "What makes you say that?"

Bridget shrugged her shoulders. "You don't seem to be afraid of anything. I would like more of your courage."

Flattered and touched, Eve patted Bridget's hand. "You already have it. You just haven't used it very much. You would be surprised at what you can accomplish without me," Eve said.

Bridget stared at her curiously. "Whatever do you mean? That almost sounds like a goodbye and it bloody well better not be," she said. "Of course you're not leaving. You love the horses and me too much to leave," she said and laughed.

Eve couldn't find it in her to correct Bridget. Soon enough she would break the news. For now, she understood her role. Support Bridget during this appearance.

"I have some great clothes for this," she said. "I just hope it all comes together."

"Just be your encouraging self. I bet you'll be surprised at how well it goes," Eve said.

"You really believe that?" Bridget asked.

"I really do," Eve said.

Minutes later, they pulled in front of the old building that served as a community center. Eve noticed groups of young men hanging out on several corners and wondered if Chantaine had gang problems. She shook her head at the thought. Hopefully not.

Once inside, Bridget was introduced by the community center director and she delivered her speech. She also listed several scholarship opportunities and Eve helped to distribute information sheets and applications to the large group. Then the fun began. Bridget, Eve and several other volunteers helped the young women select outfits.

After two hours, it was time for Bridget and Eve to leave. Eve was pleased to see the expression of satisfaction and enthusiasm on Bridget's face.

"Can you believe how excited they were?" Bridget asked as they stepped outside the building to wait for the limo to make its way to the curb. "And not just about the clothes. They really seemed curious about the scholarship opportunities and—"

"Hey, Princess, must be nice living in the castle," a young man from a large group called as they moved closer. Too close, Eve thought. "When we have nothing."

Suddenly the group rushed them. From her peripheral vision, Eve saw Bridget freeze. Her guard was opening the limo door. Eve acted on pure instinct.

"Go!" she yelled at Bridget, giving her a hard push

toward the limo and throwing herself in front of the angry group. She felt a jab in her side. Pain rocked through her. Then, another in her chest. It took her breath. She caught the flash of the fist an instant before it hit her in the forehead. Then everything went blessedly black.

"There's been an emergency with the princess, sir," his aide, Pete, said, pulling him from a meeting with a top state official.

"Emergency?" Stefan echoed, his heart sinking. "Who? Bridget or—"

"Princess Bridget, sir," his aide said, clearly trying to keep his composure. "There was some sort of stampede at the event she and Ms. Jackson attended this afternoon."

"Eve," he said, feeling his gut clench with fear. "I need details immediately," he demanded.

"I have an incoming call from the princess," his aide said, touching the Bluetooth on his ear. "Princess Bridget wants to speak with you," he said, handing Stefan his phone.

"Stefan, she was crushed," Bridget said, sobbing. "That gang came out of nowhere and rushed us. She pushed me away and stepped in front of me and there was nothing I could do," she said, sobbing between phrases.

His blood turned to ice. "Where is she?" he asked.

"On the way to the hospital." Her voice broke. "Oh, Stefan, what if she doesn't make it? What if she—"

"You can't think that way. We don't have enough information. Eve is an incredibly strong woman." He was talking to himself more so than to Bridget, coaching himself not to think the worst.

"Oh, God, I hope so. Before we arrived, she was trying to boost my confidence. It was almost like she knew she was leaving," Bridget said, her voice full of misery.

"Leaving?" he said and shook his head. "I don't know what you're talking about, Bridget. Are you sure you are okay?"

"Yes, yes, I'm fine," she said. "But Eve isn't."

"I'm going to the hospital. I'll give you an update as soon as I hear anything," he said.

"I want to go," she said.

"You need to calm down," he said. "You're in no state to be going to the hospital. I'll call you. I promise. And Bridget," he said, "I'm very, very glad you're safe."

"I love you, Stefan."

"I love you, too," he said and disconnected the phone. Pete was waiting for instructions. "Call the driver and tell him I want to leave for the hospital immediately. I'll tell Mr. Vincent that I need to reschedule the meeting."

Although it was mere moments before Stefan walked into the hospital, it had felt like hours. His mind was racing furiously. He'd called to get an update on Eve's condition and he was told the doctors were working on her and that she was unconscious. Because of her head injuries, they were concerned about swelling.

Upon entering the hospital, he was led to a private room to wait. He called Bridget to give her his limited update and was pleased to learn that she had calmed down a bit. She wanted to come to the hospital and he told her there was no use. Even he wasn't allowed to see Eve right now.

The knowledge burned a hole inside him. He paced the room and spoke with the police about the gang that had stampeded Eve. Several members were already in custody. That brought him little comfort.

Stunned that his lungs were working and that his body was performing almost normally, he couldn't remember feeling this kind of sheer terror at losing someone before. She couldn't die. He couldn't lose her.

She was the one woman who had wanted him for himself and for no other reason. She had defended him and his interests at every opportunity. She had stolen his heart.

Until now, Stefan had chosen not to project far into the future about his relationship with Eve. His position complicated things. The only thing he'd known was that he wanted to keep her as his lover and friend. Now that wasn't enough. The realization was life-changing. The advisers could go hang for all he cared. Some part of him must have known from the first time he met Eve that she was his destiny.

Staring out the window at the sunny day, he fought an overwhelming bleakness inside him. What if he'd waited too long? What if he could have somehow prevented this? God help him, he didn't know what he would do if she didn't make it.

Chapter Twelve

"Your Royal Highness," Stefan's aide said. "The doctor is here to speak with you."

"Please send him in immediately," he said.

The doctor, a middle-aged man, strode inside and the door was closed behind him. "Your Highness," he said with a quick dip of his head. "Ms. Jackson arrived with multiple lacerations, broken ribs and internal bruising. Her spleen was ruptured and had to be removed. She has also suffered a severe concussion and we're watching her for swelling. She hasn't regained consciousness since she arrived, but with the loss of blood and surgery, that's to be expected. Her condition is serious, but stable. We'll be keeping her in ICU until further evaluation."

"I must see her," Stefan said, reeling from the list of her injuries.

The doctor gave a slight grimace. "I'm not sure that's

a good idea, sir. Her face is bruised and swollen and as I told you, she's unconscious."

"I must see her," Stefan repeated, clenching his jaw.

The doctor gave a slow nod. "As you wish," he said. "Please come this way."

Stefan followed the doctor to a different floor and stepped inside the doorway of the room where Eve was surrounded by beeping machines. The sight of her in such a fragile state ripped him in half. She was so strong, so vibrant, yet now it appeared as if she were barely alive. A knot formed in the back of his throat and he forcibly swallowed it down. Her face was swollen. One of her eyes was purple.

Anger and horror built up inside him. Who could have done this to her? Why? What had she done except help his sister? In some part of his mind, he noticed that he'd clenched his fists. He deliberately released them and moved closer to her.

"May I touch her?" he asked the nurse writing on a chart just before she left the room.

"Yes. Gently," she said. "Just don't compromise her tubes or monitors."

He nodded. "Okay." Carefully, he touched the part of her arm that wasn't connected to an IV. "Eve," he said. "Hang on. I'm going to take care of you." He lifted his hand to her cheek where she wasn't swollen. "I love you. Hang on, darling. Please, hang on."

Stefan instructed his aide to update Bridget and Phillipa, and also to make sure the barns were covered. He hesitated making the call to the States to Eve's aunt because he was hoping that each passing hour would bring more hopeful news. But Eve remained unconscious. She was so still, so pale. It broke his heart to think of the pain she must have suffered when she'd stepped in front of Bridget.

He decided to stay through the night. His senior adviser, Tomas, attempted to call him repeatedly, but Stefan ignored the calls. If there were a true national emergency, then his aide would inform him. He sat in the chair next to her bed, watching her, willing her to wake up.

The next morning, she still didn't awaken. Frustration and fear battled inside him. She reminded him of a fairy-tale princess cursed to sleep.

"Is there anything else you can do?" he asked the doctor the next morning.

"We can decrease her pain medication, but we have to bear in mind that she's also recovering from emergency surgery. I know it's difficult, but sleep is giving her time to heal without being in pain. Perhaps you should go back to the palace and get some rest."

Stefan shook his head and continued his vigil next to her bed. Just after three o'clock that afternoon, he saw her stir slightly. Springing to his feet, he reached out to touch her hand. "Eve. It's Stefan. I'm here for you. We're taking care of you."

Her eyes flickered and his heart stuttered. She winced slightly and sighed, then relaxed again. "Nurse," he called just outside the room. "She moved her eyelids."

The nurse rushed inside and checked her vital signs. "Her heart rate has picked up a little. Our girl may be waking up soon," she said and smiled. "I'll check back in a while."

Still unable to relax, he paced the small room and checked on her every other minute. He took a call from Bridget and reluctantly agreed to allow her to visit later in the evening. Fifteen minutes after the nurse checked Eve's vital signs, his security guard tapped on the door.

"Pardon me, Your Highness, but one of your senior advisers wishes to see you," he said.

"Here?" Stefan asked. "He's here in the hospital?"

"He's actually waiting just outside the ICU," he said. "I can tell him you're not available, sir."

Stefan shook his head impatiently. "No, I'll give him two minutes, then be done with it," he said and strode to the hallway.

"Your Royal Highness, I've been trying to reach you all day," Tomas Gunter said.

"As you can see, we've had an emergency and Ms. Jackson has been seriously injured. What is so important that it couldn't wait until I return to the palace?" Stefan demanded.

The adviser opened his mouth, then closed it. "Sir, I believe it's best if we speak in private."

"If you can't tell me now, then it can wait," Stefan said. "Call my aide for assistance in the meantime."

Tomas shifted from one foot to the other. "Sir, as one of you senior advisers, I must tell you that your prolonged presence at the hospital is raising suspicions about your relationship with Ms. Jackson."

"And?" Stefan asked.

The adviser blinked. "Well, it isn't good for the image you've said you want to maintain to get involved with one of your staff," he said in a lowered voice.

Stefan resisted the urge to roar. "I don't give a bloody damn about my image at the moment. At the moment, the woman I love is fighting for her life. Nothing is more important. Do you understand?"

The adviser pressed his lips together. "Then you should know, sir, that Ms. Jackson had intentions of leaving Chantaine. She remained to fulfill her obligation to Princess Bridget, but she was going to leave as soon as possible."

Stefan felt as if he'd been punched. "How do you know this?"

The adviser swallowed. "I took the liberty of speaking with Ms. Jackson. I explained your goals and the importance of your reputation. She agreed that she wanted only the best for you and didn't want to be a distraction from your purpose as Crown Prince of Chantaine."

Stunned, Stefan stared at the man. "You told Eve to leave Chantaine?" he asked, trying to wrap his head around it.

"She agreed that she didn't want to compromise your future or effectiveness," the adviser insisted. "I did what I thought was best for Chantaine."

Stefan's surprise quickly turned to anger. "You overstepped your position," he said. "What gives you the right to interfere in my relationships, particularly without my foreknowledge?"

"I am your senior adviser," he said, puffing himself up and lifting his chin.

"Were," Stefan said, making an immediate decision. "You're relieved of your duties. Consider yourself dismissed."

Now Tomas looked stunned. "But, sir, I have served as an adviser since your father's reign."

"You clearly need a break," Stefan said in a crisp voice.

"You're not thinking clearly. Especially since Ms. Jackson is injured. Time will pass and you'll see that letting her return to the States is the correct path," the adviser continued.

"Not in my lifetime," he said. "You may leave."

"You'll regret this," Tomas said. "The people of Chantaine will never accept her. She has no title. She brings nothing to our people."

"How about heart, empathy and courage?" Stefan demanded, feeling his blood boil. He ached to smash his fist into the adviser's face. Glancing at his guard, he waved for him to approach.

"Please make sure Mr. Gunter is escorted to the lobby," he said, and then he returned to Eve's room.

His heart pounded with pure fury. He couldn't believe the gall of the adviser. To directly take such an action behind his back. Dismissing the man didn't seem punishment enough for what he'd done. He was tempted to strip Gunter of his previous royal commendation honors.

What must Eve have thought when she was approached by him? He wondered if she'd thought Stefan had sent him. His gut churned with the thought. He couldn't blame her for wanting to leave if she was going to have to deal with men like Gunter.

Still flaming with anger, he closed his eyes and took deep calming breaths. He suspected he would never get over his fury with the man, but for Eve's sake, he needed to get himself under control. How could he be there for her if he was ready to rip off his adviser's head?

He heard a slight rustle and turned to look at the bed. She rolled her head from one side to the other and moaned as if in pain. Rushing to the bed, he covered her hand with his. "Eve, it's Stefan. I'm here. I'm here."

She wrinkled her brow and shook her head again, fluttering her eyelashes. She blinked several times and stared at him as if she were trying to focus. "Stefan," she said in a hoarse voice. She winced again.

"What, darling? What is it?"

"Why do I feel like I've been run over by a truck?" she managed, then closed her eyes. Her face contorted in pain. "It hurts to breathe."

"That's because of your broken ribs. Rest," he said, and then punched the button for the nurse.

"My head," she said.

"Concussion," he said.

"And my gut."

"They had to remove your spleen," he said and gently touched her cheek. "Eve, I need you to know that I love you."

She grimaced again. "Oh, sweetie, that's not a good idea."

"But—"

The nurse swished into the room. "You're back, darling. The doctor will be pleased with the news. Let me check your vitals. I bet you're feeling a little rough, aren't you?"

Eve nodded and gave a pathetic sounding moan that wrenched at Stefan's gut. "She's in terrible pain," he said.

"Drugs," Eve said. "Or just shoot me."

The nurse made a *tsk*-ing sound and injected some medication directly into Eve's IV. "You poor, brave girl. This should make you feel better soon. Now rest."

Eve closed her eyes and her face gradually relaxed. Her breathing fell into a gentle rhythm.

Stefan was so relieved he sank into the chair beside the bed. "Thank God," he said.

The nurse nodded. "She's a strong woman. She's going to need to let someone else be strong for her for a while."

"She'll have that in spades," he assured the nurse.

Just as the nurse left, Bridget tiptoed into the room. "How is she?" she asked.

"Better," he said, standing to give her a hug. "She awakened for a few minutes a while ago."

Bridget's eyes lifted up. "Oh, that's wonderful. Did she talk? What did she say?"

Stefan rubbed his chin and shook his head. "She asked to be shot," he said.

Bridget bit her lip and turned to look at Eve. "Oh, my. Look at the bruises. Her eye is so swollen."

"I warned you," he said.

"I know. I just didn't realize." Bridget adjusted the sheet slightly. "It's so odd seeing her this helpless. I can't help feeling this is my fault. If I hadn't begged her to attend the event with me…"

"Then who knows what would have happened to you?" he asked, even though he understood Bridget's guilt. He had a share of his own guilt and he'd had nothing to do with the event or Eve's attendance.

"She's been such a wonderful friend to me since she arrived. Even though she's busy with your horses and doesn't party much," she said. "Being around her just made me feel—I don't know—stronger, more capable somehow. I don't know how to explain it. Please tell me her injuries will heal."

"They should," Stefan said. "They better."

Bridget glanced at him. "You're exhausted. You should go home now."

He shook his head. "I'm not ready."

She frowned. "I realize you probably feel responsible for her because you brought her to Chantaine and she has no family here, but you don't have to stay here. I can take a turn. Phillipa can, too."

"I do need to stay," he said and met Bridget's gaze. "Because I'm in love with her."

Bridget dropped her jaw and for once was speechless.

After her brief silence, she peppered him with questions, which he refused to answer. "I've told you more than anyone else knows," he said. "That's all I have to say. Right now, I'm focused on making sure Eve progresses."

Bridget studied him thoughtfully and giggled. "Well, now I understand why she wasn't at all thrilled when I was showing her photographs of the women I wanted to match up with you."

"You're not to tease her," he said sternly. "She's been through enough. What she needs right now is kindness and medication. In the meantime, give my daughter a kiss for me."

After Bridget left, Stefan stayed through the night, but he dozed off a couple of times. In the early hours, just as dawn was breaking, he opened his eyes to find Eve looking at him. Immediately rising, he went to her bedside. "How are you?"

"Floaty," she said. "If I breathe very slowly, I don't feel like screaming. My head is still—" She broke off. "Ugh."

"Can I get something for you?" he asked.

She shook her head and frowned. "Oooh, that was a mistake. No, thank you," she said in a low, hoarse voice. "How long have you been here?"

"Almost two days," he said, studying her, wanting to assure her and himself that she would be okay.

Her eyes widened. "Wow. I've been out that long?"

"You had surgery, too," he said.

"Oh. Forgot about that." She yawned and clearly

regretted it by the expression on her face. "You can go home now. I'm going to be okay."

He smiled at the way he'd given her permission. "I don't want to go home until you and I reach an agreement."

"About what?"

"About your staying in Chantaine," he said, then looked away as he tried to find the right words. "I've fallen in love with you and I need you to stay. I need and want you in my life. I realize that I'm asking a lot from a woman as independent-minded as you, but I am who I am. I have responsibilities that I can't shirk, but I don't want to live my life without you. What I'm saying is," he said, turning to face her, "I want you to—" He broke off when he saw that his heartfelt marriage proposal was falling on deaf ears. Eve had fallen back asleep.

Eve turned a corner that day and began a dramatic improvement. At least, other people considered it dramatic. She still hurt like hell every time she even thought about moving. And no one had let her near a mirror. That bothered her when she thought about it, but Bridget pooh-poohed her concerns and gently brushed her hair. Phillipa gave her reports on Stephenia. Stefan spent far too much time with her. She didn't know how she was going to tell them all that she was leaving, but she had to do it.

The day she was to be released from the hospital, Bridget arrived and applied makeup and fixed her hair. After she left, Stefan came to see her.

"You shouldn't be here," she told him. "People are going to start getting suspicious and then there will be rumors."

"No one is suspicious and there won't be rumors because we're getting married," he said.

She gaped at him. "Excuse me? Have you lost your mind? You can't marry me. I'm a commoner. I'm an American. I'm—"

"The woman I love." He wrinkled his brow. "We already discussed this. Don't you remember?"

"Remember what?" she said, searching her rusty brain. Surely she would remember this kind of conversation.

"I told you that I love you and want you by my side. I don't want to imagine my life without you. I realize being princess of Chantaine may not have been in your game plan, but I'll try to make it worth your while. I'll do my best to make you happy," he said, lifting her hand to his lips.

Her heart twisted with emotion. "Oh, Stefan, I can't. I can't do it to you. I can't do it to your future. I'll ruin you," she said and couldn't fight the tears burning her eyes.

"If what you're doing is ruining me, then do your best, sweetheart. I feel as if I'm a different man with you, and I like who that man is."

Trying to banish her hopes, she shook her head. "But you should marry someone who can help Chantaine."

"You do that," he said. "You already have."

"I mean in terms of connection or title. I really must leave Chantaine," she said.

"You need to forget that poisonous conversation you had with my senior adviser. He's been dismissed."

She gasped. "No."

"Yes. He's lucky I didn't do worse. I wanted to," he said, anger lighting his eyes. He clenched his jaw, then appeared to calm himself. "That's in the past. You and I need to concentrate on the future. You agreed to marry me, so it's settled."

She shook her head. "I did no such thing. When did we have this discussion?"

"A couple of days ago," he said nonchalantly.

She narrowed her eyes. "I was drugged. You're trying to hold me accountable for something I said when I was drugged. You're insane."

He leaned toward her, his gaze making her heart stop and stutter. "Tell the truth. Do you love me?"

She opened her mouth to protest, to lie, but the word stuck in her throat.

"Where's your courage, Eve? You face down a gang of villains for my sister, but you can't admit your feelings for me?" he challenged.

She glanced out the window, searching for strength. Her chest felt so tight she could barely stand it. "When you put it that way," she said. "I do love you. In a perfect world, I would love to be with you, but it's not a perfect world. And I don't want to mess up your destiny."

She felt his fingertips on her chin as he guided her to look at him. "You are my destiny," he said. "I know it will sometimes be difficult, but together I think we can face anything."

"I really don't see how this is going to work," she said, her eyes growing wet again. "I'm not princess material. Your people will never accept me."

"Trust me. They will," he said. "Marry me and it will be the ride of your life."

She couldn't possibly say yes. She couldn't. It would be insane, crazy… She couldn't possibly say no. "Yes," she said. "I will."

He kissed her gently and Eve clung to his hand, still not certain she'd done the right thing.

A nurse's aide arrived with a wheelchair. "Ready?" she asked.

Stefan patted beneath Eve's eyes. "You may want to check a mirror to repair—"

"Oh, the makeup," she said. "I need a mirror, please."

"Just a second," the aide said and quickly returned with a mirror.

Eve looked into it and swallowed a scream. "Oh, my God. I look like a monster."

"The swelling will go down," Stefan assured her. "You haven't seen your face before?"

"No, and I don't want to look at it again anytime soon. I need a very large pair of sunglasses," she said, setting the mirror facedown on the bedside table.

The kind aide managed to find a couple pairs of sunglasses for Eve. She chose the larger of the two and carefully placed them on her nose. The aide wheeled her down to the hospital lobby. "I hope you're ready for your fans."

"Fans?" Eve echoed and looked up at Stefan. "What fans?"

The front door opened and a large crowd applauded. Stunned, she looked at Stefan. "What is this?"

"You are Chantaine's brave heroine. My people love you," he said, helping her to stand. They walked toward the limo and were showered with rose petals.

"Viva Eve. Viva Eve," the crowd shouted.

Overwhelmed, Eve felt her eyes well with tears yet again. She bit her lip and waved, then threw a kiss.

"Just like a pro," Stefan said as they both got inside the car. "You handled your first royal appearance just like a pro."

Epilogue

Seven months later, Eve stood in an upper room of Chantaine's most historic chapel dressed in a wedding gown with a train so long it could have won a place in the Guinness World Records. She had thought it was over the top, but Bridget had insisted that the people of Chantaine wanted a grand dress for the bride of their prince. Eve was going to do her best to enjoy the affair. After all, she and Stefan had already made their own vows during a private ceremony just between the two of them. Today was a state occasion, and since she was going to be doing the princess thing, she was going to have to get used to state affairs. It was part of her role as wife to Stefan.

Even though she barely recognized herself when she glanced in the mirror, she knew Stefan was worth it all. Her hair was pulled up in front and the back of it flowed past her shoulders in waves highlighted with tiny baby's breath. The veil she wore was made of the finest Venetian lace, but crafted by local seamstresses. Her dress had also been designed by a up-and-coming local designer.

Her jewelry designer was also homegrown in Chantaine. The pearl-and-diamond drop earrings and choker had been created to complement the centuries-old tiara on her head.

"People still can't stop talking about your insistence to use only Chantaine's designers for your entire wedding. You could have had the most exquisite couture," Bridget said wistfully.

"I think our citizens did a great job. I didn't know I would be causing such a stir when I made the decision," Eve said to the small group of loving women assembled in the room with her.

Hildie, her aunt, just nodded in approval. "Practical choice. Why go to another country when you've got folks here who can do a good job?" Her aunt's face softened and she dabbed at her eyes. "Besides, she looks beautiful."

Seeing her aunt well up with emotion made Eve's heart constrict. Hildie had been there for her when no one else had been. She'd inspired her to reach beyond her situation, and Eve counted her as a huge influence on her success and confidence. Ignoring the gown, she moved to Hildie's side and hugged the woman. "Thank you for everything you've done for me. I just hope I can always make you proud."

Hildie squeezed her, then pulled back and blew her nose. "You always have."

Valentina stepped closer. "I wanted to give you this as something borrowed," she said, pressing a handkerchief into her hand. "It belonged to my great-great-great-grandmother," she said and rubbed her cheek against Eve's. "I'm so happy for you and Stefan. I can only hope that the two of you will have as much happiness as Zachary and I do."

"Thank you, Tina. The first time I met your brother, I never would have believed I would fall in love with him."

"We're all glad you did," Phillipa said. "He's a different person since you came to Chantaine."

"Thank goodness for that," Bridget muttered, then smiled. "He's happy. You're happy. The baby's happy. Now if I can finally get my year in Italy…"

Eve lifted her hands in surrender and laughed. "Not my area," she said. "You and Stefan will have to negotiate that one."

A knock sounded at the door and Bridget ran to open it a crack. Since the ugly stampede all those months ago, Bridget had become very protective of Eve. "Oh, it's you," she said excitedly. "Just a second," she said and closed the door. "Stefan's wedding gift for Eve has arrived."

"Wedding gift?" Eve said. "He already gave me a new foal."

Bridget clasped her hands together in excitement. "This gift is a little different," she said and opened the door again. A tall man stepped through the doorway and Eve felt shock waves roll through her. For the first time in almost fifteen years, she was looking at her brother Eli. She struggled with disbelief at the same time she drank in the sight of him. He was older and broader than the slight teenager she remembered. His eyes held a few character lines, but the love she saw in his eyes was the same as always.

Heedless of her gown, she raced toward him and

put her arms around his neck. "Eli, you're here. I can't believe it! I can't believe it. How did he find you?"

"Let's just say your husband-to-be is one determined son of a gun. After I left, I sent you letters, but when I didn't hear back, I figured you didn't want anything to do with me."

A knot formed in Eve's throat. "I didn't receive any letters," she said.

"That's what I figured, after Stefan tracked me down. I didn't come here to spend your wedding day talking about me, though. I came because I wanted to be here on one of the most important days of your life. I've missed a lot of other ones and I didn't want to miss this one, too."

"I'm so glad you came. So glad you're here. We will get a chance to talk, won't we?" she insisted.

"Not as much today, but I've already promised to pay another visit after you get back from your honeymoon. You're beautiful inside and out, Evie. I couldn't be more proud of you. I'm gonna head out now. I'll see you on the other side," he said with a smile and a wink.

She kissed his cheek and stared at the door after he left, her eyes burning with tears. "I'm marrying the most amazing man in the world," she said, then turned to look at the women surrounding them. Each of them was dabbing her eyes or sniffing.

Bridget was the first to recover. "Enough," she said. "Now I must touch up your makeup." Eve was fussed over and hugged, then suddenly the women left and she was alone, filled with nerves and anticipation. Sometimes she still couldn't believe all that happened, that *she* of all people was going to be a princess and do princess things. Stefan had encouraged her to adapt the role to her personality. There was going to be some give and take, such as the elaborate dress she wore today, but Eve had begun to fall in love with the people of Chantaine, so stepping outside of her comfort zone to help make the citizens happy didn't bother her as much as it once had.

A knock sounded at the door and her heart leaped. "Yes?" she said, walking toward it.

The mistress of ceremonies opened the door and nodded in approval. "You look beautiful, the most beautiful bride I've ever seen. It's time. Are you ready?"

Eve's stomach dipped. "Yes," she said, then followed the women to the foyer of the beautiful church. An orchestra swelled, signaling her to walk down the aisle. Eve took her first steps and immediately found Stefan with her gaze. She knew people would be staring at her, watching her, and her nerves could possibly overwhelm her. Looking at Stefan gave her courage.

She walked all the way down the aisle and he took her hands and greeted her with a kiss. "How is the light of my life today?" he whispered.

"Happy and excited, Your Highlyness," she said.

Stefan smiled. "After today, when you are crowned princess, I'll be saying the same thing to you. I love you, Your Highlyness-to-be."

* * * * *

 **Harlequin**®

COMING NEXT MONTH

Available May 31, 2011

S P E C I A L   E D I T I O N

"THANKS FOR NOT TURNING ON THE LIGHTS," Tyler said. "I'm a mess."

"Not in my book." Even in low light, Alex had a good view of her yellow shirt plastered to her body. It was all he could do not to reach for her, mud and all. But the next move needed to be hers, not his.

She slicked her wet hair back and squeezed some water out of the ends as she glanced upward. "I like the sound of the rain on a tin roof."

"Me, too."

She met his gaze briefly and looked away. "Where's the sink?"

"At the far end, beyond the last stall."

Tyler's running shoes squished as she walked down the aisle between the rows of stalls. She glanced sideways at Alex. "So how much of a cowboy are you these days? Do you ride the range and stuff?"

"I ride." He liked being able to say that. "Why?"

"Just wondered. Last summer, you were still a city boy. You even told me you weren't the cowboy type, but you're...different now."

He wasn't sure if that was a good thing or a bad thing. Maybe she preferred city boys to cowboys. "How am I different?"

"Well, you dress differently, and your hair's a little longer. Your face seems a little more chiseled, but maybe that's because of your hair. Also, there's something else, something harder to define, an attitude…"

"Are you saying I have an attitude?"

"Not in a bad way. It's more like a quiet confidence."

He was flattered, but still he had to laugh. "I just admitted a while ago that I have all kinds of doubts about this event tomorrow. That doesn't seem like quiet confidence to me."

"This isn't about your job, it's about…your…" She took a deep breath. "It's about your sex appeal, okay? I have no business talking about it, because it will only make me want to do things I shouldn't do." She started toward the end of the barn. "Now, where's that sink? We need to get cleaned up and go back to the house. Dinner is probably ready, and I—"

He spun her around and pulled her into his arms, mud and all. "Let's do those things." Then he kissed her, knowing that she would kiss him back, knowing that this time he would take that kiss where he wanted it to go. And she would let him.

Follow Tyler and Alex's wild adventures in
SHOULD'VE BEEN A COWBOY
Available June 2011 only from Harlequin® Blaze™
wherever books are sold.

SPECIAL EDITION

Life, Love and Family

LOVE CAN BE FOUND IN THE MOST UNLIKELY PLACES, ESPECIALLY WHEN YOU'RE NOT LOOKING FOR IT...

Failed marriages, broken families and disappointment. Cecilia and Brandon have both been unlucky in love and life and are ripe for an intervention. Good thing Brandon's mother happens to stumble upon this matchmaking project. But will Brandon be able to open his eyes and get away from his busy career to see that all he needs is right there in front of him?

FIND OUT IN

WHAT THE SINGLE DAD WANTS...

BY *USA TODAY* BESTSELLING AUTHOR

MARIE FERRARELLA

AVAILABLE IN JUNE 2011
WHEREVER BOOKS ARE SOLD.

Harlequin *Blaze*™
red-hot reads

Do you need a cowboy fix?

NEW YORK TIMES BESTSELLING AUTHOR

Vicki Lewis Thompson

RETURNS WITH HER SIZZLING TRILOGY...

Sons of Chance

Chance isn't just the last name of these rugged
Wyoming cowboys—it's their motto, too!

Take a chance...on a Chance!

Saddle up with:
SHOULD'VE BEEN A COWBOY (June)
COWBOY UP (July)
COWBOYS LIKE US (August)

**Available from Harlequin® Blaze™
wherever books are sold.**